Blood Like Poison:
Destined for a Vampire

M. LEIGHTON

PROLOGUE

The trees were blurring right in front of my eyes, looking similarly distorted to the ones on my left and right, the ones that were flying by in my peripheral vision. I blinked to clear my sight, but it was no use. It wasn't tears that clouded my vision; my eyes were just succumbing to the continued strain of looking into the darkness around me. Without Bo's blood to augment my vision, I couldn't see any better than any other human in the forest at night. I never thought I'd care that my senses were no longer so acute, but I was really missing it now.

I knew I wouldn't be able to last much longer, but I was desperate—absolutely desperate—to get away. They weren't far behind me. The forest was a treacherous place, a lonely wooden trap for a solitary human girl. They were a trap for me.

I dashed over the uneven terrain, but I knew my progress was slowing. The scenery that had been flashing by so fast was quickly becoming clear and discernible. I could feel the numbness of fatigue invading my legs, and my lungs felt like they were about to explode.

I stumbled over a clump of dirt and then nearly fell when I stepped on a branch. My feet didn't want to cooperate. They either weren't getting the urgent message from my brain or they were ignoring it. Either way, I wasn't going to be able to run much further. And then they'd catch me.

Up ahead, I could see an area where the trees were less dense, a clearing maybe. With eyes wide open, I said a quick and silent prayer that it was the clearing that I was familiar with, the one that lay just inside the forest, near where I parked. It was hard to tell, especially from a distance. At night, with only the pale moonlight as illumination, it looked just like any other clearing, the same as probably thousands of them looked in the dark.

But if it wasn't just any clearing, if it was *the* clearing, I was almost home free. It was that thought that gave my legs the burst of adrenaline that they needed to carry me on. I picked up speed and raced for the opening, for what I hoped lay beyond it—safety and freedom.

I exploded through the trees, intending to dart across the clearing and back into the trees on the other side, when the ground suddenly disappeared from beneath my feet.

One minute I was looking at the dappled stand of pines in front of me and the next I was listening to my scream bounce of the dirt walls of an earthen tube as I fell.

I landed with a bone-crunching thud, pain shooting up my legs and into my back like dozens of sharp daggers. I tried to move, to shift my body in such a way as to relieve some of the agony, but when I did, excruciating waves radiated throughout my lower half.

Anguish first stole my breath then, little by little, I felt it stealing my awareness. I clawed at consciousness, hanging on to the dark world around me with frantic desperation. If I passed out, anyone who might be looking for me would never know where I was. If I passed out, I could die down here.

This can't be how my life ends. Not in a hole in the ground, in the dark, in the woods, with vampires chasing me. Not without seeing Bo one last time. Not without Bo...

Reality was slipping from my mind like water through my fingers, leaving me in the firm grip of memories. They tangled in my brain incoherently, jumbling together in a knot of faces and scenery.

With a resolute shake of my head, I tried to focus. On anything, any one thing that would keep me awake and alert. I thought back to the night that I lost Bo.

Though weeks had passed, the wound was still so raw that it felt like only moments had elapsed since that horrific night, the night Bo, the love of my life and a vampire, drank blood so powerful and so toxic that it killed him. Only it didn't.

Of course, I didn't know that for three horrible, heartbreaking, soul-crushing days. I'd wished for death during that time, especially at night when I'd lie in my bed, in the dark, in the quiet, thinking of Bo. Smelling him.

Those memories were so intense, I felt that despair as if it was fresh. It crept into my mind, into my limbs.

In the interest of self-preservation, I skipped ahead to the day that I went to see Lucius, Bo's vampire friend. He was a mentor of sorts to Bo. He was much older, wiser. He seemed to know things that no one else did. I'd gone to his cabin in the woods to get some answers.

I thought of that day and found that, if I concentrated hard enough, I could still smell the roses in his living room, still hear the crackling of the fire in his underground mansion.

Diving head first into the details of that day, I felt the pain fade into the background as I faded back in time.

CHAPTER ONE

"Come with me," Lucius said, walking to the door that led to the cabin's luxurious basement. "I'll tell you everything I know."

I looked at Lucius—a copper-haired, pale-skinned, very powerful vampire that I knew little about. At one time, I might've hesitated before going deep beneath the ground, deep beneath the cabin's only exit with Lucius, especially by myself. But today, there was not even a pause in my step as I followed him down. I believed he had answers that I needed—answers about Bo, information I needed more than I needed to live or breathe. I had to know if Bo was alive, no matter the risk.

When we reached the bottom of the long staircase, Lucius approached the heavy door and awakened the sophisticated lock that kept intruders out. He put his thumb to the biometric pad and then punched in some numbers. When the door popped open, he swept his arm in front of his body, signaling for me to precede him.

Once again, I was amazed by the perfectly recreated Victorian parlor that spread out before me. From the rich carpets and upholstery to the huge fireplace and ornate trim, it was like stepping back in time, back to a posh mansion in the heart of 19th-century London. It was strange to think that a man of either Irish or Scottish (I thought probably Irish) decent would favor surroundings such as these.

I crossed the hardwoods and rug to the couch where Bo had lain the last time I'd been in the room. I couldn't contain the shiver of pleasure that coursed through me when I remembered his teeth sinking into my throat, his body pressed to mine. I knew I'd never survive if I couldn't feel him again, couldn't touch him, couldn't smell him.

Perching on the edge of the cushion, I pushed those thoughts aside and asked without preamble, "So, what's going on?"

"Bo's alive, am I right?"

My heart sank. "That's what I came here to find out. I thought you knew."

Lucius wagged his head back and forth. "I suspected."

"That Bo didn't die?"

"Among other things."

"Such as?"

Lucius sighed, walking to a wet bar that stood discreetly in one corner of the room. "Where to begin?" he asked absently, turning a tumbler upright and dropping three ice cubes into it with a delicate clink, clink, clink.

When his pause stretched on and it didn't seem as if he was going to speak, my impatience got the better of me. It was either prompt him or let loose the frustrated scream that had been clogging my throat for several hours now.

I began with what I felt was the most important question.

"Why do you think Bo's alive? How did he survive?"

Slowly, almost too slowly, Lucius poured amber liquid from a crystal decanter into the glass. I wanted to hit him in the head with it.

Finally, he spoke.

"I never believed the stories, lass. I always thought they were nothing more than myth. Conjecture. Fairy tales."

"What stories?"

Lucius carried his glass to an armchair that faced the couch on which I sat. Gracefully, he sank into its deep seat, crossing his legs and resting his elbows on the thickly padded arms.

"For hundreds of years, vampire legend has spoken of a man, a boy really, who cannot be killed, a boy that God Himself commissioned with the destruction of vampires, or at least one in particular. Of course, this boy's existence was never confirmed. In over two thousand years of vampire history, no one has ever seen or met this fabled creature. You can imagine that, after a while, he's become something akin to a ghost story."

Lucius paused, swirling the golden liquid in his glass, staring into its shimmering depths. When he didn't continue, I spoke.

"So, what? You think Bo is the boy who can't be killed?"

Lucius looked up at me, an inscrutable gleam in his sparkling emerald eyes.

"It's certainly a possibility."

"But why would you think that? I mean, you've only known Bo for a few years. What would make you think he's that boy, that he survived that fight with Lars?"

"For one thing, I went back for Bo's body and it wasn't there."

"Should it have been?"

"Of course."

I had wondered about that, what had happened to it. That night, when the first ambulance had arrived and the EMTs had set to work on Savannah, I'd walked back to the spot where Bo and Lars had fallen. I'd wanted to touch Bo's invisible face one last time, but their bodies were no longer there. I had just assumed that they'd turned to dust and blown away, disintegrated or something, like in the movies.

Then an alarming thought occurred to me.

"What about Lars? Does that mean he's—"

Lucius started shaking his head, interrupting me. "No. I moved his body so that the police wouldn't discover it."

"Oh," I said, relieved. Then, when what he'd said really sank in, a kernel of nervous excitement began to grow in my belly. "So Bo's body wasn't there?"

"No, lass."

"So he *is* alive?"

"I believe so, yes."

I laughed, a sound that, even to my ears, bordered on the hysterical. I couldn't help myself. My relief was that profound.

I closed my eyes, a shaky smile still on my lips. "Thank God," I whispered.

Suddenly, I felt like crying. A lump formed in my throat, but it was a happy lump, as were the tears that I felt burning the backs of my lids. I'd never felt such overwhelming gratitude.

"But that's not the only reason I think Bo might be the fabled boy."

Lucius's words brought me back to the present. I knew what he was saying was important, relevant, and that I should pay attention, but it was hard. Nothing seemed to outweigh the importance of the news I'd just been delivered. Nothing. Bo was alive; that was the only thing I really cared about.

"What else?" I asked, clearing my throat.

"The first night I met Bo, the night he turned up on my front porch, he wasn't human."

"I know. He'd just been bitten."

"No, lass, he wasn't human, but he wasn't newly turned either."

"He was already a vampire? How is that even possible?" Lucius merely watched me, silently. "How could he not have known that? How could his family not have known?"

"I believe his real family, whoever and wherever they are, did know."

"You think his parents, the Bowmans, aren't his real family?"

"That's exactly what I think."

"But his nickname, Bo, it's too—"

"A coincidence, plain and simple."

"That doesn't even make any sense. You can't just fake an entire life, an entire history."

"You can if you have very powerful blood," Lucius said, looking at me meaningfully.

Pieces started sliding into place and I gasped. There was only one really powerful vampire that I knew of, and I had no doubts that he was both capable enough and evil enough to perpetrate such an atrocity.

"Lars."

I remembered the way Lars was able to influence my mother and Trinity, the effect he had on people without even trying. I couldn't imagine what he might be able to accomplish if he put forth more effort, put forth more thought and energy, more planning into his deception.

Lucius bobbed his head indecisively. "Eh, possibly, but I was thinking of someone even more powerful. This person would have to be able to control the memories of not only humans, but another vampire as well. And, if Bo is who I think he is, he himself is very powerful. It would take someone incredibly old to subvert him."

"Wouldn't they have had to feed Bo blood in order to do it?"

"Yes."

"But I thought it was kind of an ongoing thing? I mean, three years is a long time. Wouldn't they have to feed him blood continually, over the years?"

"Yes, they would."

"Well, then how could someone have been feeding Bo vampire blood without his knowledge? And his mother, too?"

"It wouldn't be as hard as you might think. Bo's mother would've been the easier target. Humans always are. And she worked at the hospital, correct?"

"Yes. Why?"

"Well, if someone was rendezvousing with her fairly regularly, enough to keep her under their control, then that same person could've been infecting the bags of blood she was taking to Bo."

"Oh," I gasped. "I didn't even think about that."

Such ruthlessness, such impossible blackness. The person who could plan and carry out such a heinous deception would have to be evil incarnate.

"Who would do something like that? Who *could* do something like that?"

"Someone like an elder probably, someone powerful beyond imagination."

"You knew many of them, right?"

"Well, I knew *of* them. I'm not that old. The elders walked the earth long before my time."

"Any idea which one could've done something like this?"

"That, I'm not sure of, but I intend to find out."

"Do you think this could have anything to do with Heather?"

Just before Bo "died," he'd asked me to pass a message along to Lucius, the name of someone he believed to be connected to his father's death. That name was Heather. No last name, no other information—just Heather.

"I suppose it's possible, but there's only one way to know for sure."

"Find Heather."

Lucius nodded. "Find Heather."

"Well, where do we start?"

"Why don't you let me worry about that? You have a life to live. Besides, lass, I'm much more...*resilient* than you," he teased with a wink.

"I'd like to help if—"

"I know you would, and if there's something that you can do, I'll be sure to let you know."

Somehow I doubted that, but I really had no other choice but to let him do his thing. I had no idea where to even begin to look for a vampire named Heather, much less how to do it without getting myself killed in the process.

"What about Bo? How do we go about finding him?"

"That's up to Bo, lass. He's staying away for a reason. My guess is that it's to protect you."

"From what?"

"More like from *whom*. If Bo's thinking the same thing I am, he knows that the vampire we're dealing with is trouble with a capital T. Very dangerous. That's not someone he'd likely want you involved with."

"But I'm already involved. He can't *un*involve me."

"No, he can't do that, but he can surely try to keep you well-hidden from here on out."

"Well-hidden? But I'm not hiding."

"To a certain extent you are. The less contact you have with Bo—the less you are exposed to his blood—the less likely it will be that any other vampire can identify you, at least not without a very close encounter."

"But he doesn't have to stay away from me to accomplish that. All we have to do is *not* drink each other's blood. That shouldn't be too hard," I said. But then, when I remembered that Bo would no longer have the poisonous vampire blood softening his thirst, I reconsidered. "At least not for me."

"Even if Bo's thirst is not an issue, it's still not that simple."

"Why not?"

"It's not my place to tell you that. Some things, you need to hear from Bo."

"Well Bo's not around so—"

"He will tell you in his own time and that's all I will say."

Both his tone and his expression brooked no argument.

"Isn't it my decision anyway, whether or not to endanger myself?"

Lucius merely shrugged.

I wanted to rant and rave and bluster, to tell Lucius that nothing mattered except being with Bo. No risk was worth being apart from him, but I knew arguing would do me no good. It wasn't his decision, wasn't his fault. It was all up to Bo. I had no choice but to wait for him, wait for him to decide the time was right to come back to me.

Disgruntled and aggravated, I stood.

"Well, I suppose I'd better get to school. They're watching attendance more closely than ever since all the recent disappearances and accidents."

That's what all the vampire activity had been labeled by both media and law enforcement—"disappearances" and "accidents."

Lucius rose as well, walking with me to the door.

"Please do come back and visit, Ridley. I'd like to keep in touch, especially if you hear from Bo."

I was perturbed. Lucius had irritated me. *He* was supposed to be the one giving *me* answers, telling me that Bo was alright and how to find him, not the other way around.

I nodded and smiled, a gesture I knew was tightly polite. I wasn't feeling particularly warm at the moment.

****

My conversation with Lucius plagued me for several days. I couldn't help but wonder if he was right, if Bo was some kind of prophecy-fulfillment that had been colossally duped.

The only thing I knew for sure was that I needed to see Bo, needed to talk to him, and the only way I knew to do that was to catch him visiting me. So, one night I went to bed, determined to stay awake long enough to nab Bo as he came into my room.

As I lay there, listening vigilantly, I began to fantasize about seeing Bo again—touching him, talking to him. I thought of his silky dark hair, his nearly-black walnut eyes, his perfectly-carved lips. It gave me cold chills just to think of feeling those lips on mine and hearing his voice again.

I hadn't had any contact with him since the night he'd come to my room after his supposed death, an incident that I was more convinced than ever was not a dream. But I remembered every detail about him as if I'd seen him only hours before. They were permanently etched into my mind, onto my heart.

From the night he'd visited me after his "death", I'd awakened at some point every night since with his indescribably soothing tangy scent swirling in the air around me. But there was never any sign of Bo, though. Each time, I'd cut on the lights and walk the room, looking for him, reaching out with all my senses. The neighbors probably thought I had insomnia. But never, not once, did I find any trace of Bo, no evidence that he'd been there except for the smell in my nostrils and the ache in my heart.

Tonight, however, I was determined to stay awake, all night if need be, until he visited. I wanted to catch him red-handed. Even more than I wanted answers, I wanted, no *needed*, confirmation that he was alive. I needed to touch him, to feel his cool skin beneath my fingertips. I needed to know that he was out there... somewhere.

It was during my fight against sleep that it occurred to me that I could always visit Denise Bowman, Bo's mother. It was possible that I might be able to glean something from her reactions and the way she spoke about Bo, like whether or not she was still grieving and if she knew he was alive or not. Even if she didn't, she might hold valuable answers, whether she was aware of it or not.

The next morning, I woke to the persistent buzz of my alarm. I growled at the ceiling. I'd fallen asleep.

I rolled over and buried my face in the pillow, smothering a scream of aggravation. My irritation was impossible to maintain, however, when Bo's mouth-watering scent wafted up from the material and teased my nose. It was strong, as if he'd lain there at some point, resting his head on the pillow beside mine. I wondered if he'd laid down beside me while I slept. The thought was as thrilling as it was frustrating.

It did serve to improve my mood, though. My body seemed to know what my mind only suspected. Bo had held me during the night, and the knowledge of that, the elation of it was enough to keep me going for a little while longer, until I could see him again.

After I showered and dressed, I realized that I had no idea how to get in touch with Denise Bowman. What little I knew of her was that she worked third shift at the hospital, which meant that, even though I hated to intrude so early in the morning, my best chance of catching her would be after she got off work. Like right about now.

I rushed through the rest of my morning ritual and hit the door at a run. I drove at breakneck speed to Bo's house, determined to intercept Denise before she crawled into bed for the day.

The driveway at Bo's small white cottage curved around and stopped right in front of the back door. So when I pulled to the top of the drive, I could see the rear bumper of Denise's blue Volvo peeking out from behind the house.

Pulling to a stop just short of the wagon, I shut off the engine and sat inside my cooling car watching the kitchen window for signs of life. I could see that a light was on, but I didn't know if that meant she was still up or she had just forgotten to turn it off. But then I saw a shadow pass in front of the glass, so I got out and walked to the front door.

As I raised my hand to knock, I thought I heard hushed voices and something scooting, like maybe a chair or some other small piece of furniture being moved. Whoever was inside quickly quieted, however, so I just shrugged it off and rapped my knuckles lightly on the metal part of the screen door.

It only took a few seconds for Denise to answer. When she pulled open the heavy wooden door, she smiled in greeting.

It wasn't quite the smile that I was expecting. It seemed a bit tight, like maybe she was irritated. I wondered if she wasn't very happy to see me.

"Hi, Ridley," she said, opening the screen door and motioning me inside.

I was relieved that she remembered me. But before I let that encourage me too much, I reminded myself that her memories of me weren't important. It was Bo they were after, Bo they were trying to erase. If Lucius's theory was true, that is.

"Hi, Mrs. Bowman." I stopped just inside the living room and turned to face her.

"What brings you out so early?"

"I hope I'm not bothering you. I wanted to catch you before you went to sleep."

Leaving the front door open, Denise only moved a short distance into the room, hovering near the exit as if she was hoping this wasn't going to be a very long visit. I tried not to let her body language dissuade me.

"Well, you did. What can I do for you?"

Right down to business, I thought.

Luckily, I'd rehearsed a bit of what I was going to say, although it seemed that most of my planning was for naught since she was intent on rushing me.

"How are you doing?" I watched her face carefully, gauging her reaction.

"I'm fine. How are you?"

That answer didn't tell me much. It could've meant that she was putting on a brave face. It could've meant that she knew Bo was alive. It could've meant that she was taking enough drugs to kill a horse in order to cope with her grief. But it also could have meant that she wasn't grieving at all.

"I'm doing better, I guess."

She looked at me blankly, nodding her head as if she didn't know what to say.

"Actually," I began. "I wondered if you had any baby pictures of Bo that I could use for school. With all the...disappearances and stuff, we're doing a Halloween masquerade to raise funds for a memorial and I thought it would be nice to have some baby pictures of everyone to put into the slideshow at the end of the dance."

I watched Denise's brow wrinkle in confusion. Her expression said that she was searching for some meaning in what I'd said, but she was finding none.

"Bo?"

"Yes."

"Bo," she repeated, this time as if she was trying to recall something about the name, as if she was trying to remember where she'd heard it. Her own son's name. Supposedly.

With a sinking feeling, I realized that it was highly likely that Lucius was correct in his suspicions. It appeared that Denise Bowman was not Bo's mother.

"Your son, Bo," I added helpfully.

"Bo," she said again. Then, as if light was dawning, she must've latched onto a memory, whether real or fake I couldn't know. "Right. Bo. Oh, um, let me see. Maybe there's something in his room."

She walked past me toward Bo's room. Quietly, I followed. Denise stepped through the doorway and just stood staring at Bo's bed as if she'd never seen it before.

Confused, she looked around, taking in the dresser and the chest then glancing back at me.

"Do you think there would be something in here?"

I felt my eyes widen in uncertainty and disbelief. *She* was asking *me?*

"Maybe. I'm happy to help you look," I offered uncomfortably.

"That would be great."

Reluctantly, Denise walked to the dresser and slid open the top drawer. She rifled through the contents like she was picking through the clothes of a stranger, which is what I suspected that Bo was to her—a stranger.

With a sigh, I turned to rummage quickly through the night stand and then made a show of going through the chest while she fumbled through the rest of the dresser drawers.

Even though I was pretty sure I already had my answer, I wanted something more.

"What about a baby book or a photo album from when he was little?" Those were the kinds of things that almost every mother had.

I saw Denise's back stiffen.

"I can look," she replied vaguely.

After we finished canvassing Bo's room, I followed Denise back out to the living room, to a shelving unit that held the television. At the bottom were two cabinet doors, which she opened. Inside were several photo albums. She pulled out the first one she came to and turned to hand it to me.

"You can look through this one. I'll look through the rest."

Taking the album from her, I turned to the couch and perched on the edge of a cushion. I ran my hand over the brown leather cover of the book then traced the gilded letters that read *Family Photos* with my fingertip. Beneath that, someone had used black permanent marker to pen numbers, obviously the year.

The cover creaked as I opened it, a sure sign that the album was not viewed very frequently. I flipped page after shiny plastic page looking for any indication that Bo had been a part of the Bowman family before three years ago, but I found none. All the vacations and Christmases, the birthdays and picnics, were all devoid of Bo, of anyone other than Denise and her husband.

Though I was bothered more than I cared to admit, my heart broke a little for Bo. I wondered if he knew, if he'd somehow found out about the farce. But then I wondered how I could ever tell him if he hadn't. It would break his heart. Bo genuinely loved his father, or at least he thought he did. It would hurt him to know that none of it was real. It would be like losing him all over again. Whether they were or not, to Bo the memories felt real, real enough to die for.

I closed the book and rested it in my lap, glancing over to watch Denise search for a lie, for something that wasn't there, something that never had been.

Finally she looked up, tears in her eyes, and she said, "I'm so sorry, Ridley. I can't even remember what he looks like."

Standing, I carried the album back to the cabinet and put it back where it belonged. Gently, I took the other one from Denise's fingers and put it away as well.

"It's alright. I'll find something else. I think you need some rest. I bet you've had a long night."

Though she looked distraught, there was a confused blankness in her eyes that made me feel incredibly sorry for her. Someone had used—unthinkably, cruelly used and abused—her mind and her emotions in ways that no one deserved. It was a violation, an assault of the worst kind. She'd been tricked to love a son that wasn't hers and, for a while, she'd grieved the loss him, all on top of the loss of her husband. Now, she was lost, confused, and hurting, and she didn't even know why.

I said my goodbyes to Denise and left so she could go to bed, all the while my anger was mounting. Someone out there, some monster, was wreaking havoc on people's lives and whoever it was had to be stopped, had to be punished.

I was behind the wheel, my Civic's engine purring quietly in the morning fog, when an idea occurred to me. Quickly, I got out and ran back to the front door and knocked.

Once more, I thought I heard hushed voices and movement inside. Gingerly, I opened the screen door and leaned in closer, hoping to hear more clearly. More than anything, I could hear Denise's voice as she spoke softly to someone. The voices quieted for a moment before someone other than Denise spoke in a tone loud enough for me to discern.

The voice was deeper than Denise's, but still unmistakably feminine. It was hoarse and husky, bringing to mind images of Sharon Stone or some other sultry older woman.

I knocked again and waited, but there were no sounds to indicate that Denise might be coming to the door. The polite thing would've been to leave, to let Denise go to bed or tend to her secret visitor, but I wasn't feeling particularly polite so I knocked again, this time snapping my knuckles harshly on the wood.

After another full minute or two, Denise finally answered the door. A lightly sweet, floral smell—rosy almost—drifted out through the open door.

My smile was bright with apology. "I'm sorry to bother you again, but—"

"Pardon?"

"I know you were getting ready for bed, but I wanted to…" I felt my smile fade as I trailed off. A spooky thread of apprehension slithered down my spine as I looked into Denise's puzzled periwinkle eyes. It only took a couple of seconds for me to realize that she had no idea who I was.

Clearing my throat, I stumbled on. "I'm sorry to bother you. I think I have the wrong address."

I smiled again, a quick twitch of my lips, before I turned and nearly ran off her porch.

Once inside my car again, I sat looking at the house, wondering whether or not I should have tried to get inside, to see who was in there with her. Obviously, it was a vampire. Someone had managed to completely erase me from her mind in a matter of minutes. They weren't just trying to erase Bo; they were trying to erase all evidence that Bo ever existed, including those who knew and loved him—people like me.

If they (whoever "they" were) thought Bo was dead, they'd need to go back and clean up their mess, cover their tracks. I drew a small amount of comfort from that—the idea that if they thought Bo was truly dead, they might stop hunting him and trying to kill him. Right on the heels of that encouraging thought, however, was one a bit more troubling. What if *I* was a loose end that needed to be tied up as well?

Throwing the gear shift into reverse, I sped down the driveway and made my way to school. Hopefully it was true what they say: there's safety in numbers.

****

That night, I lay in bed, once again thinking of Bo and all that I'd learned. I seemed always to think of Bo, to crave him, to need him like I needed food and water, like I needed any essentially sustaining things. It was getting harder and harder to drag myself through the days knowing that I probably wouldn't see him, and it was getting harder and harder at night to believe that it really was him that I was smelling in my room. As time marched on, his presence was becoming more surreal, like my mind and my heart were colluding to play a cruel trick on me.

I clung to the story that Lucius told, if nothing else than as a possible explanation and confirmation that Bo was, in fact, alive. Tighter and tighter I held onto that as I felt him slipping through my fingers. I couldn't—I just knew that I couldn't—survive losing him again, even if I'd never really gotten him back in the first place. Hope was the only thing that had kept me living this long.

Besides, it was looking like Lucius was right. Evidently Denise was not Bo's real mother, which made Lucius's theory even more plausible. But how to set Bo free? What could I do to make things right in his life, to give our love a fighting chance?

I covered my face with my pillow. Sometimes I wondered how Bo could stay away, how, if he loved me as much as I loved him, he could go hours and hours without seeing me, talking to me, touching me. I would've given anything just to be close to him for five minutes, to feel his nearness, that familiar tug. I needed something to hold on to, something to get me through until...I don't know when.

Suddenly, I was aggravated, aggravated by the whole situation—by Bo and his determination to protect me, his concern for my safety, his willpower to stay away from me. Angrily, I threw my pillow aside and stared furiously at the ceiling.

"Bo, if you can hear me," I said, speaking aloud, wishing there was some way Bo might be near enough to hear me. I couldn't tell anymore. I couldn't feel much in life but for the agonizing hole in my heart that was ever widening. "I need to know you're here, that you're *anywhere*. Please. If you love me, I need to know that you're still out there."

I listened and I waited. I breathed in large gulps of air, testing every particle for the scent that haunted my every waking moment and most of my sleeping ones. But there was nothing, nothing but the smell of the night air that hung outside my window.

Disappointment coursed through me. It was so poignant that I could almost taste it, bitter and thick.

Maybe I was kidding myself. Maybe I'd taken denial to a whole new, unhealthy level. Maybe I was delusional.

Unable to hold back the tears that seemed always to lurk on the horizon, a sob eked out right before the first drop fell. I wondered if I'd ever have a dry pillow again. It seemed to be wet more often than not of late. I wondered, too, if I'd ever be whole, ever feel complete again. I doubted a positive outcome for either.

"Bo, please," I whispered.

At times, I could remember with perfect clarity what his arms felt like around me, what his lips felt like against mine and it tore at my guts. If I could bear to give up my memories of Bo, I would pray for amnesia, anything to quiet the way my heart constantly throbbed for him. "If you hurt like I did, you wouldn't do this to me, you *couldn't* do this to me."

My heart was breaking for the millionth time, something I didn't think was possible when the pieces were already so small they were like sand or dust. But it could happen. It happened to me all the time anymore. It's like my heart no longer knew any other mode than devastation and misery. My deluded hope was the only reason I got out of bed in the mornings, the hope that today might finally be the day that I got to see Bo.

I turned on my side and drew my legs up to my chest on the off chance that it might help hold me together, might keep me from falling apart. But it didn't. I still felt like pieces of my insides were breaking off and forcing their way out through my stomach.

And then I felt it.

Before I even smelled anything, a ripple of recognition washed through my belly. I grew instantly quiet and turned my face toward the ceiling to inhale. Like the comfort of a cool breeze on a hot day, a citrusy smell tickled my nose and I felt the mattress dip at my back.

I turned over and reached out. Though I could see nothing more than the wall and the window beyond my bed, my fingers made contact with a familiar form, with an arm I felt like I knew as well as my own. I'd dreamed of it. I'd dreamed of every inch of Bo. Every tiny detail that I could remember, I'd rehearsed over and over and over in my mind. And now he was here.

CHAPTER TWO

Before I could even speak his name, I was in his arms. Relief and happiness like nothing I'd ever felt, like nothing I could describe, flooded every fiber of my being. It washed over me, washed through me, carrying away all the doubts, all the heartache, all the pain. It was true. It was real. Bo was alive and he'd come back to me.

"Where have you been?" I muttered, the words barely intelligible as they slipped past lips that were pressed to Bo's neck.

"Not far," he said quietly. "Never far."

I felt tears of joy running down my cheeks. I'm sure he could feel them, too, the wetness against his naked skin.

His naked skin? I thought.

The idea of Bo's unclothed body so close to mine—in my bed, in the dark—was like setting a match to dry grass, grass deprived too long of the nourishment of rain. Flames of desire tore through my body like brushfire, incinerating all thoughts, all feelings, but for my need of Bo.

Since he held no visible form, I closed my eyes and pictured him in my head. Leaning back, I pressed my lips to his, using nothing more than my vivid memories to guide me. Unerringly, they found the smooth contours of his mouth.

Bo felt stiff, but I didn't care. I'd dreamed of his lips, of his kiss and his touch, for what seemed like an eternity. I didn't care about anything else, any consequences or repercussions, and I had no intention of giving up on the moment I'd waited for so long.

Determined, I kept my lips pressed to his until I felt them soften. It was nearly imperceptible at first, but it wasn't lost on me. I saw my chance and I took it.

Pushing my fingers into his hair, I lay across Bo's lap, pulling him down into a deeper kiss. His cool breath was brushing my cheek in short, heavy pants. It was then that I knew that he still felt it too, that he still wanted me as much as I wanted him. He was just resisting it. But I wasn't going to let him. I needed this. I needed him, his passion. I needed him to lose himself to me the way I'd long ago lost myself to him.

Bo remained strong despite his rising desire. Though he was no longer so stiff, I could tell that he was holding back, clinging tightly to his control.

I ached to be closer to him. My body throbbed for his touch. I craved him on a cellular level that screamed from the tip of every nerve, from every square inch of my flesh. Some untouched, primal part of me begged for a completion that only Bo could give me. I didn't know when I'd see him again; I just knew I had to get my fill of him tonight.

Determined to push him over the edge, I flicked my tongue across his lips and pressed my heavy breasts to his chest. I sensed the pause in him, like a gasp that I could feel rather than hear. He stopped breathing for a split second.

His struggle, his indecision, was a nearly palpable thing, as was his burning fervor. I knew the instant that the first teetering domino fell and Bo lost the battle. But his loss was my victory. It meant I got what I wanted.

In the blink of an eye, Bo's resistance gave way to a flood of emotion, bathing me in what I yearned for most: his passion. It exploded onto me and stole my breath, setting my blood on fire.

Without hesitation, without caution, Bo's tongue stormed my mouth, slipping inside to lick and tease mine. Gripping my waist with his big hands, Bo lifted me, guiding my body until I was straddling him.

Roving my back and my hips, Bo's hands brought to burning life everything they touched. As he gripped my ribs, his thumbs grazed the sides of my breasts, sending pulses of pleasure rocketing through my body to the place where our bodies touched most intimately.

He moved beneath me, his need violent. I wiggled atop him, dying to get closer, my need equal to his.

Then, as if he suddenly realized he was spiraling out of control, the tempo of his ardor changed, slowing to a sensually languorous onslaught.

Bo's palms came to a rest on my hips, his fingertips sliding under the edge of my panties. As his tongue slid rhythmically in and out of my mouth, Bo's hands dug into my flesh, pulling my soft body firmly against his harder one. My insides melted into boiling hot lava that pooled between my thighs.

I couldn't contain the moan that flowed from my mouth into Bo's. His answer was a deep purr that sounded in the back of his throat, vibrating along my nerves and stirring my very core. Goosebumps skittered across my skin.

Bo's lips left mine and blazed a trail across my cheek and jaw, down to the tender spot beneath my left ear. I arched my back, begging for him to take what I knew he wanted. I could feel his thirst for me, for my blood, for my body, as if we'd never been apart, and I reveled in it.

And the flames raged on.

Against my neck, I felt the scrape of something sharp— his teeth. I knew that if I could see him, his eyes would be a pale, pale green and his skin would be nearly translucent, showing the fine network of vessels just beneath its surface. He would have four sharp canines, two on the top and two on the bottom, begging for the flesh of my throat, for the rich red fluid that pumped through my arteries.

Then suddenly, without warning, Bo pushed me away and I found myself sitting alone in the center of the bed, confused. Gone was Bo's cool skin, his closeness, the wildfire of his passion.

I looked around my bedroom, searching for his shimmer. But again, I saw nothing.

"Bo?"

Though he didn't answer, I knew he was still with me. Even if I hadn't been able to hear his heavy breathing where he stood somewhere in the shadows, I would've known he was near. I could still feel his presence like pulses of sweet electricity humming through my veins, like some part of him was actually inside me.

"Bo, what's wrong?"

"This is why I have to stay away," he growled, every "s" a hiss in the quietness of the night.

"But why? I want this. I want you."

"Because it's not safe and I don't want to put you in danger."

His continued disregard of what I wanted, of what I cared about, of what I thought was best for me, got my hackles up for some reason.

"Then why did you come?" I snapped, coming angrily to my knees.

I heard Bo sigh as he moved nearer to where I knelt on the bed.

When he said nothing, I asked again. "Why? Why did you come to me then?"

There was a long pause before he answered.

"Because I can't stay away," he confessed softly, tucking a stray lock of hair behind my ear. "Even if you can't see me, even if you don't know I'm around, I have to be close to you. But tonight, I got too close. I wanted to touch you so badly that I- I..." He trailed off, regret evident in his voice.

I grabbed his wrist and pressed my cheek into his palm. "Can't you understand that I feel the same way? It's killing me not to see you or talk to you or touch you."

Air hissed through Bo's teeth with his sharp inhalation. "But I'm a danger to you like this. I'm weak right now and the smell of your blood, of your body all warm with desire." He groaned. "I'm afraid I'll hurt you."

"You won't hurt me, Bo. I trust you not to. Besides," I said shuffling closer to him. "You won't do anything to me that I don't want you to."

"That's not the point, even though it should be. You should be afraid of me, of what my bite could do to you. But even if you're not, if we exchange blood, it could put you in the crosshairs of whoever's doing this to me. And I won't have that. I can't have that."

Both his words and his tone were final. I knew there would be no changing his mind, no matter how much I argued.

"Why can't you feed and come to me when you're not so…so…thirsty."

"For one thing, I don't have a steady supply from the blood bank anymore."

I thought about his mother, but I said nothing. I didn't want to broach that deep and painful subject at the moment.

"Can't Lucius get you some?"

"He might be able to spare a little, but I've stayed away to protect him, too."

"Bo, you can't do this alone. There are people who love you, who want to help you, and you have to let us."

Bo rubbed his thumb across my lips and, though I couldn't see him, I thought he was probably smiling, a tiny, sad quirk of the lips.

"You're amazing, did you know that?"

"Bo, I'm serious."

"I know you are, and I hope it won't be much longer until we can be together."

That brought me a modicum of consolation, but it still sounded like a goodbye-for-now kind of deal, which set off a pang of dread in my stomach.

"Don't go," I said, preempting him. "Stay. Just for a little while longer."

"I can't, Ridley. I can't fight this much longer."

I wanted to tell him not to, not to even try to fight it, but I knew it was no use. His mind was made up and I'd just have to wait until he felt it was safe to come again.

"When will I see you again?"

"Soon," he answered vaguely.

Bo leaned forward and pressed his lips to my forehead. The tender gesture soothed my frazzled nerves like a calming tide.

He pulled back, but didn't walk away. I imagined that he was staring down at me and I looked up to where his eyes probably were.

I knew that, in mine, he could undoubtedly see the fear, the desperation, the love, the raw need that tore at my heart.

"I love you, too" he whispered, as if reading my mind.

My chest felt like it was going to explode when I heard him turn to walk away. How could one moment in time be so bitter and yet so sweet?

Sitting back on my haunches, I listened until I heard nothing but the soft shift of my curtains as the breeze ruffled them and the nighttime symphony that played just outside my window.

I closed my eyes and inhaled. His scent was strong. It clung to my hair, to my skin, to my lips. I hugged my arms around me, feeling at the same time empty and full. It was with those conflicting feelings that I finally drifted off into the best sleep I'd had in days.

****

"The Accident."   That was the generic name that the public at large had adopted to identify the singular event comprised of Bo and Devon's disappearance and the brutal assault on Savannah.

It was during the weeks that followed "the accident" that I began to see a marked difference at school. In a good way, it was like stepping into The Twilight Zone—a whole other world. There had been many changes, but one of the biggest (and the best as far as I was concerned), however, was that people were actually sort of nice to each other. I know, crazy, right?

Trinity, the resident evil-doer, had turned into a vampire and fled school, taking with her a toxin that had plagued her peers for years. She had essentially traded in one kind of venom for another, only the venom she could spread with her fangs hadn't become as proliferative. Yet.

Though everyone undoubtedly thought she went missing (like Bo and Devon), I think they were shamefully relieved that she was gone. With her out of the picture, it was as if a dark cloud had been lifted from the student body. Despite the disappearances of a few in our number, the mood was lighter than I'd ever known it to be.

I could really see the burgeoning love in everyone's response to Devon. He was Trinity's ex-boyfriend, one she'd attacked and absconded with the night of the accident. Despite his history with Trinity, everyone liked Devon. It was even more apparent now. There were always flowers at the foot of his locker and pictures of him hanging all over the door. It was a fabulous show of love and support, a loud statement saying he was dearly missed. I thought his locker looked more like a memorial. What it said to me was that, deep down, everyone suspected that Devon wasn't coming back.

The atmosphere had gotten even better last week when Savannah had made her first appearance at school since "the accident." She'd suffered a traumatic brain injury at the hands of Trinity and had lost her sight as a result. Savannah had no memory of it, so no one but me knew exactly what had happened, that Trinity had been involved.

Since being released from the hospital, Savannah had been schooled at home. But last week she'd stopped by to get lesson plans from her teachers to take to her tutor. It was the first time most people had seen her since the accident, and her presence energized students and faculty alike.

Savannah's amazing recovery and brave face were just what the doctor ordered for morale. The school had a new hero, one with flaming red hair and a quick smile.

With the fall of a villain and the rise of a hero, one could only expect that the vacuum created by the absence of Trinity would soon suck something else in to fill its void—or in this case someone else.

Trinity's particular brand of evil had left a hole in the student body, and more and more it looked like a replacement was already on the way, and that replacement was Summer.

Summer had been what could be loosely described as my best friend until Bo came along. Our relationship had never been very typical of that sort of designation, though. I simply viewed her as the lesser of the evils among the cheerleaders. I never fully trusted her or told her anything important. I just hung out with her more than the rest, I suppose, which wasn't really all that much.

Though I knew she'd always been a reluctant follower of Trinity, she was a follower nonetheless. For that reason, I couldn't be totally surprised by her strange metamorphosis. Trinity had that effect on people and she'd almost hand-picked Summer to be her right-hand girl.

I always started thinking about Summer close to lunch time, the most dreaded twenty minutes of my day. I hated lunch for many reasons. Without Savannah, Devon and Bo at school—the trio that had become my official lunchtime mates—I'd been informally inducted back into "the group" by Summer. She all but insisted that I eat lunch at their table again, something that was only made more uncomfortable by the presence of my ex, Drew, the guy I'd dumped when I'd begun developing feelings for Bo.

I used to be a person who would've gone along just to keep from rocking the boat. But now, my reasons for going along were much different. I knew that if Trinity returned to Harker (if she'd even left), she would likely make an appearance to someone from that group, and the best way to stay on top of the situation was to stick close to those people during lunch. That's when I could pick up on the latest gossip and learn who was doing what, when and with whom.

"What are you doing this weekend, Ridley?" Summer asked me, jarring me from my thoughts.

Her smile was pleasant enough, but it didn't reach her eyes like it used to. She was much…different since Trinity's disappearance. She was colder somehow, stony and pretentious. Insincere.

"Dad's coming home, so I'm sure he'll have something planned," I answered vaguely. I gladly latched onto that excuse. The last thing I needed was attention. I wanted nothing more than to stay under the radar.

Besides, it was true: Dad would be home for the weekend and I'd have to play my part in our family production of The Family That Pretends They Didn't Lose a Member. It was an ongoing performance that you could find at my house every weekend. It was one that had been initiated when my older sister was killed in a car accident more than three years ago.

"Too bad. I was thinking of planning a pre-Halloween horror fest, starting with a bonfire in the woods right outside Arlisle Preserve. I think that would be an awesome way to start the weekend of our Halloween Masquerade Dance."

Several of the wannabes at the table ooh'd and aah'd at the scary genius of Summer's plan. I had hoped that with Trinity gone, people at this school would begin think for themselves a little more, not be such blind followers of the popular kids. But, alas, it wasn't to be so. I suppose once a follower, always a follower.

"Do you think that's really a good idea, Summer? I mean, they still haven't caught the Southmoore Slayer and you know Arlisle Preserve is where most of his victims have been found."

Summer rolled her eyes. "Like one guy's really going to attack a huge group of high school kids, Ridley."

What she didn't know is that the murders were being committed by a band of rogue vampires called Uccideres, not by one human serial killer as the police thought. Just one vampire could easily take out many, many unprepared teenagers, but I couldn't very well tell her that.

"Yeah, Ridley. Paranoid much?" Aisha said from down the table, turning to giggle with Carly. They were both cheerleaders and quite possibly two of the biggest followers of them all.

"Just remember that when you have to go into the woods to pee, in the dark, by yourself, Aisha," I taunted with a quirk of my brow.

Aisha's head whipped around, her mouth agape and her eyes round. Her look plainly said that she hadn't thought of that.

"That's what I thought," I said smugly, unscrewing the lid to my Coke and taking a swig.

I used to sit quietly by and let life play out around me. All I used to want was to keep my head down, graduate with honors and get a cheerleading scholarship to Stanford. I had to smile at how much had changed in such a short amount of time.

"Anyway," Summer said pointedly. "Who's in? Who's not afraid of their shadow?"

Several people snickered and almost everyone agreed to Summer's plan. What it sounded like to me was that they were agreeing to jump off of whatever cliff Summer chose. The whole thing made me sick to my stomach. It made the loss of my lunchtime *compadres* even harder to swallow than usual, and that was pretty hard.

I pushed my way through the meal, dreading cheerleading practice more and more as the day wore on. It was becoming increasingly difficult to pretend that my life was here with these people, people that I nearly detested sometimes, because it wasn't. My life was with a guy that I hadn't truly seen, not with my eyes, in weeks.

My heart ached with thoughts of Bo. I missed him more than I ever thought I could miss another human being. Well, quasi-human being. I would've gladly given up...well everything to see him just one more time.

Since that night, when his visit had ended up turning steamy, Bo had kept a safe distance. I knew he still checked in on me; I could smell him. Sometimes I even thought he might be watching me from not too far away during the day. Sometimes I suspected he was somewhere fairly close watching me during practice. It was like a tugging deep in my belly, like my body wanted to go to him, wherever he was. I never did see him, though, not even his shimmer. He was careful to remain undetected. Though I found it incredibly frustrating, it was, at the same time, an amazing comfort just to know that he was still with me.

I'd long since discovered that the best thing I could do was keep busy. An effort to do exactly that (keep busy) is what prompted me to change my course on the way home from practice. At the last minute, I decided to pay Savannah a visit.

Though I'd gone to see her in the hospital during her recovery, I had never been to Savannah's house before. Luckily, it was easy to find and not too far from Bo's old house.

I thought back to the first time I saw her after the accident, when she was still in the hospital. That first encounter was strange, what with Savannah still coming to terms with her new infirmity and all.

"Aren't you going to ask about all the scratches on my face?"

Savannah had been sitting up in the hospital bed, her coppery hair flipped to one side, hiding the shaved places of her scalp. She was smiling cheerfully.

"Alright, what happened to your face?"

"Give me a break! I'm a blind girl learning to eat with a fork. What did you expect?"

Shaking my head, I had rolled my eyes. I was discovering that Savannah's primary coping skill was humor, humor that I suspected was a clever cloaking device for denial. Of course, I didn't think any of the jokes she had told on that day were funny. They were all blind jokes that made me incredibly uneasy.

"How am I ever going to find a boyfriend like this, Ridley?"

At that I had looked up, my heart going out to her.

"Savannah, I—"

"A blind date, dummy," she'd cackled.

By that point, I had become downright uncomfortable with her "coping" and that joke in particular struck a nerve.

Savannah's jovial expression had straightened after a minute and her smile had died. Though her chocolate eyes stared blankly past me, I could see a deep sadness filling their luminous depths. Without her having to say a word, I knew what she was thinking. I had been thinking the same thing.

She had cast her eyes down as if she was staring at her covers, where her fingers picked anxiously at the material of her bleached white sheets. "Still no word about him?"

She had been referring to Devon. He and Savannah had just begun their relationship when Trinity had attacked them. No one had seen or heard from him since. The trail was ice cold and the police had no leads. I alone could've pointed them in the right direction, but they would've carted me off to the loony bin within five minutes of arriving at the station.

I suppose I could've told Savannah what I suspected might have happened to Devon, but somehow I thought that might only further traumatize her, knowing that her boyfriend had most likely died a terrible death at the hands of a vengeful vampire.

"No, but they're still looking. No one's giving up."

Dejected, Savannah had simply nodded. "I'll never give up hope."

"None of us will."

Savannah cleared her throat before moving on to a subject slightly less painful for her, though at that time, it had been one infinitely more agonizing for me.

"No word about Bo either?"

Now, as I cut the engine in Savannah's driveway, I almost felt guilty about what had happened since that conversation. No longer did I have to torture myself with worst-case scenarios about what had become of Bo, nor did I have to look ahead to a future without him. I knew he was alright. For the time being anyway.

Shaking off that thought, I got out and walked up to the red front door of the little gray house that was Savannah's. I knocked and waited.

When no one answered right away, I began having misgivings about showing up unannounced. I was turning to step off the front porch, intending to just go on home instead, when I heard the pop of the front door unlocking.

An older man stood behind the screen. He had black hair with sprinkles of gray at the temples and piercing chocolate eyes, eyes that I recognized. They were the exact shade of Savannah's. He was handsome, but I could tell that, other than the eyes, Savannah must've gotten her looks from her mother.

"Can I help you?" he asked pleasantly.

"My name is Ridley. I'm a friend of Savannah's. I thought I'd stop by and see her, but I can see I should've called first..." I trailed off, feeling ashamed of my inconsiderate behavior.

Savannah's life had been turned upside down even more than mine had. I'd lost a sister. Savannah had lost her mother, her boyfriend and now her sight. She totally got the prize for worst luck ever.

"Don't be silly. Savannah would love to have a visitor. I'm Jeremy. It's nice to meet you, Ridley," he said, opening the screen door and holding it wide. "Come on in."

With an answering smile, I accepted his invitation. On the surface, it appeared that Jeremy, or Mr. Grant as I would always think of him, was dealing with the loss of his wife and Savannah's sight in a much more healthful way than my family had dealt with the death of my older sister, Izzy.

"She's back in her room," he explained, leading me through the living room. "Vanna!"

From somewhere toward the back of the house, I heard Savannah respond. "Yeah?"

"You've got company."

"Be right there."

Mr. Grant led me into a cozy den that sat just off the kitchen. It was a bright room with sliding patio doors that dominated one wall. The other wall was bricked from floor to ceiling. A wood-burning stove was set into it and above that hung a big flat screen.

"Have a seat. As you heard, she'll be right out."

With a wink, Mr. Grant turned toward the kitchen and resumed what I imagined were supper preparations. He had peeled a mountain of potatoes that sat on the counter beside the sink.

"Would you like to stay for dinner, Ridley? I'm making my famous loaded baked potato soup."

"Thank you, but my parents are expecting me."

Though that wasn't entirely true, it was what came to mind first, so I went with it. I hated to impose on them any more than what I already had.

"His soup is hardly famous anyway, right Dad?"

Savannah appeared at the mouth of the hallway. She walked slowly, but without any assistance other than the fingertips that she trailed along the wall to her right.

"But it will be, o ye of little faith." Again, Mr. Grant winked at me. I liked him already. I imagined that their household was one of love and laughter and, for that, I envied Savannah.

"Yeah, yeah," Savannah said, making her way to the couch where I sat. "What's up, chickie?" she asked, her smile as bright as ever.

"I'm thinking of ditching school and eavesdropping on you and your tutor until graduation. What do you think?"

Savannah laughed, the same easy tinkle of delight I'd come to expect from her. "That bad, huh?"

"Eh, could be better," I answered. "Don't get me wrong. It's nowhere near as bad as when Trinity was there, but I get the feeling it won't be long until we're right back to square one."

"Why? Who's the evil dominatrix now?"

"I'll give you one guess."

"Aisha."

I thought about her answer. For many reasons, Aisha would've been the logical choice. She had the attitude for it. "Actually, it's Summer."

"Summer? She's a mindless freak."

"Savannah!" her Dad chimed in warningly from the kitchen.

"Fine, she's a mindless follower. I never would've expected her to have the spine for Trinity's spot."

"It is weird, isn't it?" And it was. The more I thought about it, the more I had to admit that it was very surprising.

"I'm so glad you stopped by," Savannah said suddenly, throwing her arms around my neck with startling accuracy.

My guilt disappeared as if it had never been, replaced by happiness that I hadn't turned around and gone home.

"Come on," she said, standing and grabbing my hand. "Let's go back to my room where nobody will be listening." She added that last a little louder, directing the words over her shoulder toward her father.

I looked back at Mr. Grant where he stood in the kitchen. He was smiling, shaking his head. Tolerance and affection were virtually dripping off of him. It was plain to see that he loved his daughter very much.

Down the hall, I followed Savannah through the second door on the left. She stopped just inside the doorway to say, "Out, Kitty."

A second later, a knee-high, ball-of-fur white dog bolted past me.

"Was that a dog?"

I marveled at the stupidity of my question. Of course it was a dog, but…

"Yep. He's four and he's a pest."

"But, it's a dog."

The intellectual quotient of the conversation seemed to be going downhill at an alarming rate.

"Right."

"Did you just call him 'Kitty'?"

"Yeah. I got him as the subject of an experiment on psychological warfare between mammalian species."

My mouth dropped open. She'd named the dog "Kitty" as a psych experiment on mammals?

Savannah walked on into her bedroom before stopping in the center of the floor and turning back to me. Then she started giggling.

"Nah, I'm just kidding. I thought it'd be funny to name a dog 'Kitty'."

I had to laugh. What else could I do?

Savannah's room was everything I might've expected from someone with her effervescent personality. Her white-framed bed was covered in a black satin comforter that had bright yellow pillows all over it. There was a huge sunflower stenciled on the wall above the bed and in its center was a collage of pictures. Her curtains boasted wide black and yellow stripes, just like a bumble bee, and in the corner there was a desk. It was painted fire engine-red and surrounded on both sides by concert and movie posters.

Looking around, I felt like I would need a sedative if I stayed in there too long. But then I spotted a tranquil island in the midst of the storm that was her room. It was in the form of an armoire.

Painted plain white, its doors were ajar and inside were dozens of framed pictures, arranged haphazardly on the shelves. The silver, gold and pewter frames gleamed in the sunlight streaming through the windows and drew me like a soothing mirage.

I walked to the cabinet and looked through the images. There were pictures of Savannah throughout her childhood doing various things, things like holding trophies, swimming in a lake, sitting on a horse and shooting a basketball from the free-throw line. There were pictures of people I assumed were friends and family, people dear to Savannah's heart. Among the lot, there was even a picture of me and Bo, sitting beneath the big tree at school where we ate lunch sometimes. That one made me ache, made my heart hurt. I missed him so much.

But among the hodge-podge of prints were several images of a woman. She was a recurring theme in many of the pictures. She was quite beautiful, with long wavy red hair and skin like porcelain. Her smile was bright and happy just like Savannah's. There was no mistaking that she was Savannah's mother, though she could easily have passed for an older sister now.

My heart went out to Savannah. I recognized this kind of pain, recognized the signs of it, of wanting to hang on to every little piece of someone who was never coming back. In my mind, in my heart, our house looked like Savannah's room—memories and pictures of Izzy everywhere. The reality of it, however, was a whole different story.

My family acknowledged neither the one-time presence of Izzy nor the loss of her. Her bedroom, which Mom kept exactly as Izzy had left it, was the only outward indication or reminder that she'd ever been a member of our family. Other than that, there was no evidence that Izzy had ever existed. No random pictures or scattered memorabilia. But inside, deep down in the places that hurt the worst, the places that missed her the most, there was no escaping the pain of it. That's something that would never go away, no matter how much we tried to hide it.

"Do you believe in ghosts?"

At Savannah's question, I turned to look at her. She was perched on the end of her bed, her legs drawn up beneath her, staring blankly at the wall in front of her.

"I don't know. I've never really thought about it. Why?"

Savannah hesitated for only a second before she answered. "Since the accident, I've seen her."

"Seen who?"

"My mother."

I looked back at the pictures. There were several things I wanted to say, but how to say them delicately was beyond me.

Clearing my throat, I said, "Your mother, um, passed away, right?"

"Yeah. She drowned a little over four years ago."

I nodded. That's what I thought. "And you've been seeing her?"

Savannah nodded. "I know. It's crazy, right?"

I said nothing, but I was thinking that it pretty much was.

"It's her, though. I know it. It even smells like her, like roses."

"Do- do you think you might be imagining it?"

"No," she replied emphatically. "I can see her perfectly, like crystal clear. I can see her just like I could if I had my sight back. That clearly."

"Does she ever, uh, speak or anything?"

Savannah's expression fell a bit. "No. Not yet. When she comes back, I'm going to talk to her, see if she'll tell me what she's doing here."

"What does she look like? I mean, can you tell that she's…"

"That she drowned?" Savannah supplied. "No. She looks just like she always did. She hasn't changed one bit." Her tone was almost wistful and I felt sorry for her.

During those days when I thought Bo was gone, I imagined that I smelled him everywhere. The mind can play cruel tricks on you when you want something so badly.

I looked back to the shelves of pictures. Not knowing what else to say and becoming more and more uncomfortable with the silence, I picked an image to ask about.

"So, did you actually win this talent contest?"

"Which one?"

"The 'Tweens That Rock' one."

Savannah smiled, her easy smile, the one that said we were moving on from the subject of her ghostly mother. "Of course I did. How could you question my ability to rock a stadium, even at age nine?"

I laughed and purposefully steered the conversation into happier, less creepy waters..

CHAPTER THREE

When I got to the house, Mom was home, which was truly bizarre. Trepidation tickled my spine. The last time she'd been home when I'd gotten there was when Lars had exchanged blood with her and made her a totally different person for a day or two. Not that she was a bad person during that time. In fact, I wouldn't have minded having that woman around more often, just not like that, not under those circumstances.

In some ways, Mom was very predictable. Monday through Thursday, she went straight to O'Malley's after work and didn't usually get in until after 10:00. Sometimes it would be really late, like midnight or so. Apparently it was a time consuming process, getting your drink on; that's why she got a jump on it at, like, 5:15.

For dealing with life after the death of a child, memory eradication via vodka was Mom's coping skill of choice. I would've liked to stage an intervention long ago, but I couldn't do that by myself and Dad was no help. Since Izzy's death, he'd never disembarked the denial train. I doubted he even admitted to himself that Mom was a drunk.

He just avoided it, like he did most things in life. He traveled all week long and we played at being the perfect family on the weekends. End of story.

The front door was unlocked and I walked in cautiously. From the kitchen, I could hear the clank of spoon against pot and I was immediately suspicious. Mom didn't cook unless Dad was home and she was in her pretender mode.

"Ridley? Is that you?"

"Yeah, Mom."

"Come in here. I've got some good news for you."

Uh-oh, I thought.

Setting my duffel in the floor, I walked into the kitchen, bracing myself for what I might find. Turns out, it wasn't all that bad. Well, maybe I should say it wasn't all that unusual. Mom was stirring a sauce pan. She was making herself an enormous hot toddy. She liked them when she felt a cold coming on.

"Are you sick?"

On cue, Mom sniffled. "I think I'm getting a cold. I have a tickle in the back of my throat and my nose has run all day. I thought I'd nip it in the bud."

I loved her rationale for drinking. According to Mom, drinking alcohol, which has been scientifically proven to actually lower the immune system, is the answer to warding off a cold. Of course, I had to give her credit. She was rarely ever sick, unless it was Smirnoff-induced. I didn't think many germs could live in a pure grain environment, which is what undoubtedly flowed through her veins.

"Have you eaten? Do you want me to fix us some supper?"

"That's sweet, honey, but I think I'll drink this and go to bed early."

"Okay." I was turning to walk to my room when I remembered what she'd originally said. "What was the news?"

"What?" Mom swung around to look at me, clearly puzzled. "Oh, right. One of my clients is the new Professor of Mythology at USC. His name is Sebastian Aiello—Doctor Sebastian Aiello—and he's looking for a sitter for his daughter. Just for the occasional evening and maybe some weekend work until the holidays. He asked if you'd be interested."

"Since when do I babysit?"

"Since someone offered to pay you twenty dollars an hour to babysit."

"Oh," I said, perking up. Suddenly, babysitting didn't sound so bad.

"That's what I thought," Mom said, a knowing look on her face. She turned back to her bubbling libation. "He said there's some kind of function that he has to attend tomorrow night and he'd like—"

"I have a late practice tomorrow night."

"—and he'd like for you to come over about 7:30, after your practice."

"Oh," I repeated. "Okay. Where does he live?"

"In Mont Claire. The address is on the back of the envelope I put on your dresser."

Mont Claire. That was a ritzy neighborhood. Of course, I have no idea how much college professors make, but it must be good money. At least I'd be babysitting in style. Plus, I'd be padding my bank account for...well, for whatever happened after graduation. I used to save for life at Stanford, but now I had no idea what to expect out of the future. Heck, I didn't even know what to expect from the next ten minutes sometimes.

Life sure has gotten a lot more exciting and unpredictable since I met Bo, I thought.

Before I left the kitchen, I looked back at my mother. She sniffed again. "Thanks, Mom."

"You're welcome, Ridley."

I took one last look at her back, one last longing look at the person I wish I saw every day, rather than the one that I cleaned puke off of once or twice a week. I almost wanted to hang around and enjoy her, but it would make the return to status quo that much more painful, so I left.

****

Something woke me. My heart leapt as soon as my mind came fully awake. I had been eagerly anticipating the next time I'd catch Bo in a visit. I knew he came, but I hadn't talked to him, touched him, felt him since that one amazing night when he'd held me in his arms and kissed me like he couldn't help himself.

I inhaled deeply. A sweetly fresh smell set off a series of alarm bells somewhere in the back of my mind. Even if my nose hadn't detected it, my body already knew that my visitor was not Bo. My muscles were tight with apprehension and my pulse throbbed in fear. Thanks to the burst of adrenaline, my vision was crystal clear, even in the dark. Not that it mattered. I couldn't make out anything. My visitor was invisible. That meant that my visitor was a vampire, and by the smell, I assumed it was a female vampire.

I sat up and scooted back until my shoulders were flush with the headboard. My breath came in quick pants and my ears strained to pick up the slightest indication of where the vampire might be in relation to my bed.

Other than my nose, my senses picked up absolutely nothing until a low growl split the quiet just before something hit me from the side, knocking me over on the bed.

Someone was on top of me, someone incredibly strong and incredibly determined. My arms were bent at the elbow defensively, my forearms covering my face. I struggled ineffectively against the vampire and those few seconds felt like an eternity to my battered body. Then I felt the brush of hair at my shoulder.

Instinctively, I pushed at the face that now hovered at my neck. I heard the snapping of teeth and I leaned as far away as I could get from that mouth.

I squelched the scream that crouched in my throat. I couldn't risk my mother's life by alerting her to the danger that I was in. I kicked and flailed as much as I could without exposing my throat to the razor sharp teeth that I knew were bared. I didn't have to see them to know that they were there. The fact that the vampire was invisible told me that she hadn't fed recently. That meant she was most assuredly after my blood.

She wrapped her fingers around my wrists, easily subduing me.

"Shhh," she hissed. "It will only hurt for a moment."

I struggled all the more. Her answer to that was to turn me onto my belly and stretch out on top of me, all in one smooth motion that happened so fast it made my head spin.

My arms were pinned beneath me. My legs were completely useless against her. I bucked my hips, but she held me down with what seemed like no effort on her part whatsoever.

She brushed my hair aside and curled her fingers around the collar of my t-shirt. I heard the ripping of cotton as she yanked, tearing my shirt open nearly to my waist.

I felt the tickle of her hair as she leaned forward. I held my breath, waiting, knowing that I was completely at her mercy. In my head, I screamed out for Bo, wishing that I could somehow call him telepathically.

The sharp sting of her teeth entering the tender flesh just above my left shoulder blade assured me that it was too late for help, even if Bo did somehow hear me. I felt the separation of muscle from bone as she pinched the tissue between her four teeth and closed her jaws. Within seconds an intense burning sensation began to seep into the skin and muscle surrounding her fangs.

I was frozen in fear.

Much sooner than I expected, she rolled me over onto my back again. She must not have drunk very much because she was still virtually transparent. Now, though, I could make out the faintest of outlines, just enough to determine that my attacker was, in fact, a woman. A very petite woman.

Eyes wide with terror, I watched the clearish shape move. It appeared that she raised her arm to her mouth. I heard the sickening squish of teeth entering flesh as she bit into her own wrist. It was followed by the popping sound of tendons tearing.

She leaned toward me again, but stopped with her arm hovering over my face. I felt one drop of cool fluid splatter against my cheek beside my mouth. I turned my face away and squeezed my lips shut as tightly as they would go.

I expected her to force me, but she didn't. She was perfectly motionless for a few seconds before I felt her tense and then spring from the bed. I heard the soft sounds of her dashing across the carpet toward the window and scurrying through it.

Her escape was nearly silent as she scampered across the yard. When those soft sounds faded, there was nothing. I sat up in the bed and rose to my knees. The silence lasted for only a few seconds before I heard more movement, heavier movement. Despite my fear and shock and the fire that burned where she bit me, a familiar tugging in my gut told me that the source of the sounds this time was Bo.

I listened intently, waiting for his approach, my body already begging for him to come closer. I heard his steps stop for an instant before they rushed off.

My heart sank. I'd thought he was coming to me, but it sounded like he had changed his mind.

When I heard his retreat stop, my anticipation rose once more. There was a pause, as if he was hesitating, maybe taking a moment to decide what to do. Then, much to my pleasure, I heard his footfalls as he hurried back toward the house. With my pulse pounding in my ears, I almost missed the nearly-silent sounds of him coming through my window.

The wind carried Bo's heady scent to my nose first. As I inhaled, I felt a calm steal over me, a peace, a comfort that only Bo's presence could bring. I could have cried with relief.

He padded quietly to the bed.

"Where?" he asked sharply.

At first I was confused, the intensity of his nearness so poignant I was nearly stupefied.

"Wh- what? Where's what?" I asked blankly.

"Where did she bite you?"

My mind was still reeling, a bizarre disorientation muddying my thoughts.

"I- I don't know..."

"Ridley," Bo snapped, taking me by the shoulders. He shook me lightly. "Think! Where did she bite you?"

Though my head was abuzz, Bo's grip on my shoulder reminded me that the area was painful.

"My left shoulder," I managed sluggishly.

Quickly, Bo came around and knelt behind me, pushing me forward. I felt his chilly fingers at my back and goose flesh raced across my skin. Despite everything else, my nipples tightened in response to his touch.

"Ridley, focus," he spat, the "s" making that familiar hissing sound. "Stay still. I have to suck the venom out before it spreads, before it's too late."

At that moment, I didn't care what Bo did to me. I felt oddly detached from my mind, and my body was virtually numb but for the feel of his big hands on me, his cool breath fanning my naked skin and the intense burning at my shoulder.

Once again, he gripped my arms, and then I felt the piercing nip of his teeth. It wasn't nearly as painful as the female's bite had been. Whether because of my desire for Bo or simply his tenderness, I couldn't be sure, but it was much less unpleasant when he did it.

Only the sounds of Bo's sucking broke the silence. After several minutes, my mind began to clear and the discomfort receded, giving way to a strange tingling sensation.

The night air, flowing unchecked through the window, had cooled my room. As Bo drank, the increasing heat of his body scorched the chilly skin of my back. Besides his rising body temperature, I could feel other changes in him, too, changes that made my heart dance and my stomach flutter. The way Bo held me, the way his lips moved across my skin, I knew that he was no longer entirely focused on the venom.

He was tasting my blood in his mouth, feeling my body against his.

Little by little, Bo's fingers loosened their grip on my arms and his thumbs began to move, drawing small circles on my skin. I felt the silky whisper of his tongue as it licked at the flesh of my back.

Bo's desire was on the rise. It was like a tangible presence in the room with us. When he shifted closer to my back, pressing his chest against me and bending his body over mine, a wave of heat gushed through my body. I could feel every hard inch of him rubbing against my back side.

The knock at my door jarred me back to reality. The heat of Bo at my back was gone just as my bedroom door opened.

Mom didn't even open the door enough for me to see her face; she cracked it just enough to ask, "Ridley, are you alright?"

My wits were slow to return, as was normal breathing. I couldn't hide my breathlessness, so I used it to my advantage.

"I'm fine. I woke up scared. Just a nightmare. Go back to sleep," I encouraged, resisting the urge to go and slam the door shut in her face so Bo and I could pick up where we left off.

"Okay. G'night," she said, yawning and pulling the door shut.

I rushed to the window, hoping Bo hadn't gone, but he had. There was no sign of him, but for the lingering scent of him in my hair and the tingle of the skin at my shoulder.

****

Throughout the next day, I wracked my brain trying to figure out why the scent of my attacker seemed familiar. I knew I'd smelled it before, but I just couldn't identify it. It was like that elusive word stuck on the tip of your tongue. It's there, but you just can't get to it.

I'd thought about her on and off all day, my attacker. I was still bothered by it, yes, but it was more an effort to keep my mind off Bo. I wanted desperately to see him, actually see him, to recommit his handsome face to memory. But deep down, I knew he wouldn't make an appearance. Not in public. Not today, not ever. He couldn't. There would be too many questions, too many inconsistencies. No, Bo would never be able to show his face in Harker again.

Acid roiled in the pit of my stomach just thinking about it, so I purposely steered my mind into more soothing waters. At least I could still feel him; that always made things seem better.

Once or twice, I'd sensed his presence. I knew he was...somewhere, somewhere close, but I never did catch even a tiny glimpse of his shimmer. The one time I'd actually seen him in his translucent state, I'd seen the way the light bent around his invisible form. It had been like looking at the trees through the heat waves that roll off of hot pavement. I found myself continually watching for that distortion, any visual confirmation that he was out there. Somewhere.

But, in the end, I knew I'd have to content myself with just knowing he was near, with feeling the tug of his presence on my heart. It would be a while before things got back to normal, and even then, it wouldn't be in this town.

Bringing my mind back to the present, I rolled to a stop at the red light. I was on my way to Dr. Sebastian Aiello's house and I was not having an easy time finding it.

I glanced down at the two sets of directions in my lap. One was a handwritten note in my mother's neat cursive. The other was a print out from Google Maps. Neither seemed to be taking me exactly where I wanted to go. It was almost as if the address for my new employer didn't exist.

I expected some confusion from Mom's directions. That's why I printed a set from a much more reliable, less intoxicated source, but that wasn't doing the trick either.

When the light turned green, I proceeded straight through the light for the second time. I watched street signs to the left and right as I passed, but nowhere did I see the one I was looking for.

Frustrated, I pushed the gas pedal to the floor and zoomed past the Dead End sign, aiming to turn around and go through the directions one more time.

I swung the car in a wide right, starting to make the turn, when I saw a small road that split off behind a stand of trees. To the left of the entrance was a wrought iron sign that read Haven Drive, just the one I was looking for.

I guided the car through the trees and realized that it wasn't a street, but a driveway. It wound through more trees and then up a slight incline. At the top sat a mammoth stone home that looked like a small castle. It crouched in the center of a ring of huge maple trees that cast a perpetual shadow over the cool gray structure.

I pulled to a stop in front of the bay of garage doors, hoping I didn't choose the one he'd have to pull his car out of. I cut the engine and got out to walk to the front door.

I rang the bell. I could hear the muted majestic chimes sounding behind the heavy wood. A little chill skittered down my spine. They had an ominous ring that made me uncomfortable for some reason.

That feeling, however, was washed away the instant the door opened revealing an incredibly handsome man that I felt sure must have modeled for Calvin Klein at some point. I assumed—I hoped— that this was Sebastian Aiello.

Dressed in fitted charcoal pants and a pewter silk shirt, he looked to be in his late twenties or early thirties. At well over six feet, he was tall with broad shoulders and slim hips. His skin was like bronze, his hair like spun gold.

He smiled, a wide spread of his perfect lips that nearly stole my breath.

"You must be Ridley."

His voice was like honey and it made my brain feel like mush. He didn't inspire the trance-like fascination that Lars did, so I wasn't alarmed. He was just so impeccably, beautifully crafted, I was almost in awe.

I nodded.

"I'm Sebastian," he said. "Please, come in."

He stepped back, sweeping his hand in front of him. I obliged by sliding past him into the grand foyer.

Soft light from a massive crystal chandelier shone in the rich wood paneling and glinted off the polished stone floors. I felt like I'd stumbled into an episode of Cribs.

"I really appreciate you doing this for us. I know babysitting probably isn't the ideal way to make a buck, but I wanted someone a little older to watch Lilly."

I smiled politely and nodded, feeling more dumbstruck as the minutes ticked by.

"Come on. I'll introduce you."

Sebastian turned and guided me down a long, wide hallway. I busied myself with looking at the amazing art that lined its length so that I wouldn't get caught gawking at Sebastian's butt. I couldn't help but notice that he filled out his pants to perfection and that wasn't a thought that I felt comfortable having.

The inside of the house was as stunning as the outside. I had to concentrate on keeping my mouth shut, as it wanted to fall open in wonder several times.

All the materials I could see were either smooth, gleaming woods or rough, cool stone. From the floors to the ceilings, everything was decorated to complement the castle-like feel of the house. There was even a suit of armor standing guard outside the entrance to what appeared to be his study. I'd never seen a suit of armor before and it gave me the comical feeling of being on an adventure with Scooby Doo.

After we'd passed several doors, the corridor widened and split into two large rooms. To my right was the kitchen and behind it was a huge dining room. To my left was an informal den, outfitted with three puffy leather couches and a fireplace so big that I could stand inside it.

Kneeling on the thick Oriental rug that lay between the sofas was a little girl. She looked to be about three or four years old and she was bent over a nearly life-size doll that was rolled over onto its belly. The doll's yellow dress was hiked up over its head and the little girl was struggling to change its diaper. There was a wet spot on the white material, and I could only assume that it was one of those dolls that you put water in so that when you squeezed it, the doll would pee.

Sebastian walked to the child and squatted down in front of her.

"Lilly, she's here."

The little girl's head popped up and her face lit up like she'd just found a long lost friend.

Though she looked nothing like her father, she was just as stunning. Her auburn hair hung in long thick waves around her tiny face and her silvery eyes shone with pleasure. When I saw their pale color, I thought maybe that's what she got from her father (other than pure gorgeousness): grayish eyes. It seemed that hers were just a bit more blue.

"You're Ridley?"

I couldn't help but smile at the bell of excitement that rang in her tiny voice.

"I am."

She got to her feet and practically ran to me, taking my hand in her smaller one. "Come and see my room."

"Lilly, I need to talk to Ridley for a minute before you drag her off, ok?"

Lilly sighed. "Ok," she said, turning back to the doll she'd left half dressed.

Sebastian shook his head in that tolerant way that parents do and turned his attention back to me.

"She's already eaten and had her bath. Bedtime is 9:00, no matter what she tries to tell you. She likes a story, but she'll try to talk you into telling her a dozen, so don't be fooled. She gets one." He smiled, obviously amused by his daughter's ploys. If possible, I thought that made him even more attractive. "She doesn't usually watch much television, probably because her room is full of toys. Do you have any questions for me?"

I tried to think back to babysitting etiquette. It had been so long since I'd actually done it, I felt rusty.

"Does she have any allergies or medical conditions that I should know about?"

Sebastian's tawny brows rose.

"No, but those are good questions."

For some reason, his compliment made me feel sparkly and wonderful. I couldn't help the smile of pleasure I felt tugging at my lips.

"What about a number in case of emergencies?"

"My cell's under the magnet on the fridge."

I nodded.

"I shouldn't be too late. I know you have school tomorrow, so—"

"Don't worry about that. I'm a night owl."

"Me, too," Sebastian said, grinning. "Alright, well, I'll get going. Make yourself at home. There's food and drinks in the fridge. Just made some fresh tea. Help yourself. There are DVDs behind that shelf," he explained, pointing to the built-ins that framed the gigantic fireplace. Then, as if deciding that was insufficient, he walked toward them. "Here, let me show you."

I followed Sebastian to the left of the fireplace.

"It's hinged," he said, pulling on a discreet handle that lay at the edge of the shelf. It opened, revealing what probably numbered in the hundreds of DVDs.

"That's cool," I said under my breath, duly impressed.

"If you—"

"Daddy, just go," Lilly said from her place on the carpet.

Sebastian chuckled. "Someone's anxious to have you all to herself."

Lilly rolled her eyes in such an adult way, in such a grown-up gesture, that I had to laugh.

"I want to show her my princess castle."

"Well, far be it for me to stand in the way of that," Sebastian teased. "You two have fun. Lilly, you be a good girl."

"I will, Daddy," she promised absently then took my hand again. "Come on, Ridley."

****

Two hours, one tea (a real one for me, a pretend one for her), several hide-and-seeks and three stories later, I was creeping down the hall, away from Lilly's room, where she'd finally gone to sleep. She was much harder to refuse than Sebastian made it seem. Something about that dainty voice and those shiny blue-gray eyes tugged at my heart strings and made it virtually impossible to say no.

I stopped a ways down the hall to listen, making sure that I didn't hear her stirring or calling for me. As I strained to hear, a light in the otherwise dark room of Sebastian's study caught my eye.

I stepped past the suit of armor, giving it a wide berth, and stood just inside the doorway, peering into the dimly lit room. A wide desk dominated the space. It was stained a rich reddish color that matched the cabinetry that covered the wall behind it. The intricately carved wooden shelves held hundreds of tomes. I could make out the titles of several of them, all whimsical works. None of them really surprised me, though, since Sebastian was a Professor of Mythology. Among the many rows and rows of books, however, one collection stood out from the rest.

It was a set of books that shared a deep red spine, each having gilded lettering that I couldn't read from across the room. One book lay on a slanted platform, displayed under a light that shone on its old, leather cover. It drew me like a moth to a flame.

As I neared it, the smell of aged paper stung my nose. My fingers itched to open the dusty cover and touch the wrinkled pages. I leaned in close enough to make out the faded symbols stenciled across the front, though they meant nothing to me.

A shiver snaked its way through me and I thought I should probably get out of Sebastian's personal space, but something inside me just wouldn't let me move away from that book.

Compelled beyond reason to open it, I reached out with one finger and gently lifted the cover. The leather creaked and that musty smell wafted up to envelope me in a puff of stale air.

The first page was littered with a bunch of letters and symbols that I didn't recognize. The second page was not much better, with its smeared images that looked like a collage of small, overlapping charcoal portraits. I paid them little attention, turning to another page instead.

Line after line of markings and symbols crossed the page, filling it with words I couldn't decipher and content that I couldn't understand. I flipped through several more pages and found nothing but the same.

I was just about to close the book when a crisp white corner caught my eye. It was stuck between two yellowed pages about halfway through the book. I turned there.

On the paper was a list of the markings I'd seen on the previous pages of the book. Beside them were English words and phrases. It appeared that someone, presumably Sebastian, was attempting to translate the work into English.

I turned the page and there, tucked between the pieces of dry old parchment, was another sheet of paper. This one held sentences that I could actually read and understand.

It seemed as though the book was some sort of history of the vampire legend, a detailed accounting of where the tales had originated and how the "curse" had been passed down through time and generations.

...began with Constantine. Of all the guardian angels, he was one of the greatest in his choir. His works were many, his dedication unmatched. But, alas, as every great figure must, Constantine had a weakness, an Achilles heel. His downfall would prove to be another heavenly being, a messenger angel by the name of Iofiel.

Iofiel was the Angel of Beauty and Constantine loved her from the moment they met, just as Iofiel became enamored with him. It would only take days for their love to blossom into obsession, an obsession that would shift their focus from serving God and humanity and turn it toward one another.

This was sin in the eyes of God, an act of rebellion, for it was never His intention when He created the angels for them to love anything more than they loved God and man.

The second of their sins was committed when their duty began to interfere with their need to be together and, in direct defiance of God's will, they left their posts as angels and hid amongst man, unwilling to continue to serve humanity if it meant being separated. During that time, Iofiel conceived and bore Constantine a child, a strapping young boy.

Infuriated by their third and final act of rebellion, God dispatched dominions to return the two angels to Him. When Constantine heard of this, he hid Iofiel and their child with the humans before he left to find and kill the dominions who sought to tear their family apart. His parting words to Iofiel were promises that he'd soon return for her and their son.

Weeks and months passed, and every day, Iofiel searched the horizon for the return of her love. When one year had passed without sign of Constantine, Iofiel left the child in the care of an old woman and set out to find Constantine.

She was quickly captured by more dominions and returned to God, never to see Constantine or their child again.

When word reached Constantine that Iofiel had been taken, his rage toward God was so complete and so overwhelming that he sought to destroy Him. In his final and unforgivable act of sin, Constantine joined the dark angels of the earth, vowing to serve the one being he believed to be strong enough to defeat God—the angel, Lucifer.

As punishment, God cursed Constantine by trapping his son in a human form and imbuing him with a power that no other of God's creations possessed: the singular ability to take Constantine's life.

In answer to God's punishment, Lucifer instilled in Constantine a venom, one that was filled with dark and unnatural elements. Lucifer believed the deadly bite of Constantine would destroy the child and spare Constantine his life.

Unbeknownst to Constantine, his venom would create an aberration in the human race, a violent and blood thirsty mutation that neither time nor many weapons could destroy.

For years, Constantine searched the earth for his son, sinking his deadly teeth into anyone that thought to get in his way. As his fury drove him, the venom corrupted him, blackening his soul to a state beyond redemption. As his darkness grew, he began to target the worst specimens of the human race, turning them into a soulless band of creatures known as Uccideres.

Finally, Constantine located his son. The boy, named Boaz, had reached his nineteenth summer and was of full maturity. Constantine, still fearful of God's prophecy, waited until night had fallen to approach his son. He crept in and visited him while he slept, while the boy was at his weakest.

Constantine bit him in the neck, emptying into him a venom so toxic no mere mortal could have survived its effects. Only this boy was no mere mortal, and the venom, though it made him frightfully ill, did not destroy the child as Lucifer had hoped.

Constantine, desperate to escape death, yet unable to kill his son, fed the boy his own powerfully angelic blood and then planted false memories in his mind. He made sure that Boaz would live a life free from the remembrance of his mission until such a time as Constantine could find a way to kill him.

For centuries, Constantine and Lucifer have worked to destroy the boy, each time failing and each time being forced to provide the boy with new memories. And so the cycle will continue, as Boaz remains immortal under God's pledge that he will not taste of death until he sees his father take his last breath.

The words melted into a breathless tangle inside my mind. The story. The legend. Boaz. Constantine. Angels. The boy who can't be killed. Could it be related to what Lucius had told me? Could it be related to what had happened with Bo? Could Boaz be my Bo?

I blinked my eyes and saw dark wooden beams across a soft white ceiling. Confusion hammered at my brain. I closed my eyes, counted to ten and opened them again. Still, I was looking at the ceiling. Somewhere. And why was I on my back? I'd just been standing in Sebastian's office in front of that book. And now...

"I was wondering if I was going to have to wake you up."

I looked to my left and saw Sebastian. I sat up so fast my head spun. We were in the den and I was on one of the three sofas, Sebastian on the one across from me.

"Was it that boring? I've always loved that movie," he said, grinning pleasantly.

"Movie?"

Sebastian's brows twitched, but they didn't draw together. "Yeah. I know it predates you a bit, but I thought you might—"

"We were watching a movie?"

This time, Sebastian did frown. "Are you alright?"

"I- I'm not sure. How long have I been asleep?"

"I don't know. Maybe half an hour. I hated to wake you."

I rubbed the back of my hand across my eyes. His answer only served to exacerbate my puzzlement.

"What time is it?"

Sebastian glanced at his expensive-looking watch. It was then that I noticed he was in different clothes than the ones he'd left wearing.

"12:15."

Ohmigod! I thought. Where had the last two and a half hours gone?

"Oh," I said, trying to sound casual. "What time was it when you got in? I forgot to check the clock."

Sebastian gave me a concerned look, but said nothing about it.

"11:30."

He'd been here for forty-five minutes and I remembered none of it! We'd apparently watched part of a movie together, too.

"I guess I'd better get going then," I said, pushing myself to my feet.

"Are you sure you're alright? I can drive you if you're feeling ill," Sebastian offered, coming to his feet as well.

"Oh, no, I'm fine. But thank you."

I hated to seem as if I was rushing off, but I was so addled, I felt almost desperate to get away, to clear the fog from my mind. As I walked down the hall toward the front door, I could hear Sebastian's footsteps trailing close behind.

"Hold on, Ridley. I owe you some money for tonight," Sebastian said, coming to stand in front of me at the door. I had my hand on the knob, ready to bolt.

"Oh." I couldn't think of one good, sane reason to leave without taking the money, so I waited while Sebastian pulled his money clip from his pocket and flipped through the denominations until he came up with a hundred dollar bill.

When he handed it to me, I felt guilty for taking it. I mean, apparently I'd blacked out for the last half of my stint and then had the nerve to fall asleep in front of him. That hardly sounded like he was getting his money's worth. But arguing would only prolong the time I had to hang around, so I pocketed the money, thanked him and opened the door.

"Are you free Sunday night? It would only be for two or three hours in the evening."

I wanted to snap at him and scream, Not now! But instead, I managed to control myself enough to smile politely and say, "Can you call me Saturday?"

Sebastian nodded. "Will do."

"Alright, I'll talk to you then."

"Drive safe."

I muttered something like okie dokie over my shoulder as I practically ran down the steps toward my car. Once I was inside it, I started up the engine and backed out, racing down the driveway at breakneck speed. When I reached the bottom, I came to a gravel-slinging stop and slammed the car into park.

I rolled the window down to let the cool night air in then I closed my eyes and leaned my head back against the rest. I pulled in gulp after gulp of the chilly air, hoping the cleansing breaths would clear my mind of the cotton that seemed to have invaded it.

When I was feeling marginally more alert, I raised my head and opened my eyes just in time to see a red blur flash in front of my headlights. I looked around, hoping to catch sight of what was out there. I neither saw nor heard anything, but nevertheless, I locked my door and rolled up my window.

Just before the window sealed out the light breeze, something disturbing and vaguely familiar tickled my nostrils. It was a sweet floral scent that I'd smelled before, and not at a good time. It was the same aroma I'd detected on the vampire that had crawled into my room and attacked me.

A noise at the back of the car had me pulling the gear shift down into drive and flooring the gas pedal. I looked left and right then checked my rearview mirror, but I saw no sign of anyone or anything. But that didn't slow me down. I barely even paused until I was pulling in behind Mom's car in the driveway.

Since I'd met Bo, I'd left my bedroom window open nearly every night. Except tonight. With no idea where Bo was or how to reach him, and some kind of crazed vampire after me, I'd never felt more vulnerable.

CHAPTER FOUR

The next day, I was pleased to have the distraction of Summer's impromptu Forest Fest to dive into. Though I had no intention of going, it was all the rage at school and it's all anyone was talking about. I let myself melt into the conversations, let myself get lost in the normalcy of parties, popularity and high school in general.

That day, my ache for Bo seemed to be worse than ever. I felt detached from him in a way I hadn't experienced before and it both terrified and distressed me. That bond we shared, that connection, had been the only thing that had kept me sane since his "disappearance" and it seemed to be fading little by little as the days wore on. I couldn't help but wonder if that bite had something to do with it.

By lunchtime, I found myself sitting at Summer's table, surrounded by people I'd known most of my life, all strangers now. At least that's what they felt like. I fiddled with my napkin as I gazed longingly across the lawn to the picnic table I'd shared for a while with my friends. And with Bo.

My heart twisted painfully with thoughts of him. I slid my eyes over to the tree where we'd enjoyed several sunny days together, alone.

In the very pit of stomach, I felt that oh-so-familiar tug and I latched onto it, closing my eyes to savor the tiny tingle that danced along my nerves. I'd felt it several times lately, so I knew he was somewhere close enough for me to feel him, yet still not close enough.

But when that feeling grew stronger, more intense, I knew Bo had to be closer than usual. Sure he must've been standing right in front of me, I raised my lids to look around. I didn't have to search for him, didn't have to look anywhere but straight ahead, at the very spot I'd been daydreaming about.

The wind blew through the branches of the big tree, dappling the ground beneath it with bright spots of sunshine, and for just an instant, I saw something shimmer in the light. Knowledge and recognition swelled inside me. It was Bo. He was here, at school, watching me, closer than he'd been in recent days.

Just like he'd promised, Bo wasn't far.

I don't know why he chose that day to take such a chance. It was like he knew how desperately I needed him—to see him, even if it was only a hint of him—and he'd risked exposure to show me that he was thinking of me, that he needed to be close to me, too. Or maybe he'd felt the growing distance between us as well. I had no way of knowing.

A relief so profound it nearly brought me to tears washed over me, and I felt the renewal of our bond pouring through my veins. That one moment in time, that one instant, was enough to keep me going for a little while longer. For now, it was enough.

Carried on the wings of Bo's visit for the rest of the day, I felt bullet-proof, like nothing could bring me down. That's why later, I decided that I'd pay Lucius a visit. I needed to talk to someone about what I'd learned at Bo's house, as well as the translation I'd found at Sebastian's.

Thinking of Sebastian made me wonder again, uneasily, about the time I'd lost there. I had no idea what to make of it and I was hesitant to mention it to anyone. A tiny seed of fear had begun to take root deep inside my mind, a kernel of dread that I might be starting to experience the effects of Bo drinking from me. What if blacking out was the first step to losing your mind? The first step to what the authorities were mistakenly labeling Mad Cow Disease?

Pushing the disturbing ruminations aside, I brought my focus back to Bo and his visit. Though thinking of him did make me feel better, acknowledging my concerns about my health had still managed to dampen my spirits in a way that not even my prior elation could fix.

At home, I unlocked the door and went to change clothes before heading to the forest to see Lucius. Looking at the sparse selection in my closet made me realize that I needed to do some laundry, and what better time than on a Friday night?

"That's right, girls of the world. I lead the most enviable life imaginable," I said aloud to the empty bathroom as I separated colored clothes from white.

My words echoed flatly back to me, bouncing off the walls of the tiny room. It was then that I noticed that the other bathroom door, the one that adjoined Izzy's room, was closed, making the already small room seem claustrophobic.

As I straightened, unease raised the hairs at my nape. Walking quietly, cautiously, to that door, I grabbed the knob and twisted it slowly. When I pushed it open, I reached out with all my senses for anything amiss.

Everything seemed exactly the same as it always did. It still smelled vaguely of Izzy and, as I made my way around the room, I didn't see where anything appeared to be missing.

I let my fingers trail along the edge of the jewelry box and the decorative tops of the perfume bottles that dotted the surface of the vanity. I ran my hand over the silky comforter that covered the bed and I ruffled the curtains as I passed. When I got to the bookshelf that sat in one corner, I mentally cataloged every item I knew to have a place there. Nothing was gone.

I turned to head back to the bathroom when something struck me. I stepped back to the bookshelf and examined a silver-framed picture. It showed me and Izzy at the beach, posing in our bathing suits when we were about six or seven years old. I smiled as I took in Izzy's cheeky grin and her sparkling eyes and chestnut hair, so different from my own nearly-black hair and equally dark eyes. But then I saw the fingerprint smudge that marred the perfect sheen of the frame.

I didn't need to wonder if it was already there. I knew it wasn't. It had been left recently. Someone had picked it up to look at it and then set it back down a little to the left of where it normally sat. I could see a blank space in the dust from where the picture usually was.

Who would go into Izzy's room? Everyone in my family knew that nothing was to be touched. Ever. Whoever it was didn't belong there, didn't know the rules. And they'd gone through my room to get in, because they'd closed the bathroom door behind them.

A chill ran through me. I thought of the woman who'd attacked me the other night. Had she been in my house since then? Could it have been her? Who was she? What did she want with me? And my sister?

Taking one last look around the room, I went back for my laundry and headed to the washer, my thoughts still on Izzy.

As sisters, we'd been close, had always gotten along pretty well, which just made it that much harder when she was gone. Izzy had always been a bright spot. She laughed a lot, as did I. It was something that I missed terribly.

I smiled as I remembered that she couldn't even stop laughing long enough to record a serious outgoing voice mail message on her cell phone. She'd done well up to the very end, when she'd punctuated her greeting with a giggle.

With a sigh, I wished once more that they'd been able to find her cell phone. No one had seen it since the accident. To this day, I'd give anything to have it, to have some way to hear her voice again, to hear her laugh.

Shaking off my morose reflections, I set my basket down in front of the washer and opened it to put my clothes in. The smell of stale alcohol nearly knocked me down. Already in the washer were some pajamas and sheets. Apparently Mom had gotten sick in bed last night.

She had been in her room when I got home, so I assumed that she was sleeping off a doozy. The doozy part was right, if the smell of vodka was any indication. She must've vomited at least eighty proof.

With a sigh, I washed her stuff first. There was no way I was putting my clothes in with that mess.

When I'd finished folding the last of my colored clothes, I picked out some jeans and an apricot sweater, slipped them on and left for the forest. The shorter days meant that it was nearly dark by the time I parked by the familiar sign with the graffiti on it. I hesitated for a moment, wondering if it was really smart to be going into the woods alone at night with someone out there prowling around looking for me. But then my need to talk to Lucius won out over my caution and I hopped out and headed for the trees.

As I walked the vaguely familiar path, I prayed that Bo was somewhere near, watching out for me. I knew he couldn't be everywhere at once, and I didn't feel him, but I really hoped he hadn't gone to do something else tonight.

My head had begun to throb with the strain of the trip when I saw the small cabin come into view. I breathed a sigh of relief.

Sketchers thumping on the wooden boards, I mounted the steps to the porch and walked to the door to knock. I was a bit puzzled when Lucius didn't answer right away. With his enhanced senses, I know he'd have been able to pick up on my arrival easily.

I knocked again. Still no response.

Stepping down off the porch, I headed around the side of the small structure to see if there was a back door. I was a little anxious about snooping around a vampire's house without his knowledge, and even more so about doing it in the deepening dark, but I was desperate to find Lucius.

When I'd made my way back to the front door and was still no closer to finding Lucius than when I'd arrived, I figured it was probably time to just give it up for the night. I still had to get back to my car and the longer I waited, the more dangerous the trip became. These woods were known vampire hunting grounds and I knew the risks of running into one.

I set out across the tiny lawn that encircled the cabin then carefully began picking my way through the dark forest. I hadn't gone far from the cabin when I heard the faintest of rustling sounds somewhere out in front of me. There was a time (when I'd had some of Bo's blood) that I might've been able to see more acutely in the darkness, hear more noises in the quiet, smell fainter traces in the air, but those days were long gone. I was once more an average, un-augmented human.

I stopped to listen, straining to hear above the sounds of the frogs and crickets. Nothing seemed out of order, so I resumed my journey, albeit a bit more quickly and cautiously.

When I heard another noise, I stopped again to listen, but there was no need. It was plain to me that there was something walking toward me in the woods, dry leaves crunching under foot.

A twig snapped, and it sounded so close I jumped. My heart was pounding away at my ribs, my muscles bunched and ready for action, and I was just turning to bolt back in the direction of the cabin when I caught a familiar scent on the wind. It smelled like honeysuckle in the summertime and I knew who carried that aroma.

"Lucius?" I whispered.

"Oh, you're getting better, lass," he said from somewhere in the trees.

"Where are you?" I was peering into the darkness, but it was no use. The moon was new and the forest was pitch black.

"Here," he said.

I had no trouble seeing him when he emerged from between the trunks of two huge trees. His uber pale skin shone like alabaster in the low moonlight. And there was plenty of it to see; he was wearing a big smile and nothing else.

My mouth dropped open and I looked quickly away.

"Why are you naked?"

Lucius chuckled. "I've been hunting. Why do you think?"

"Oh."

I could feel the blood heating up my cheeks.

"Were you looking for me?" Lucius asked, coming to stand in front of me.

"Um, yeah," I said, growing more uncomfortable by the minute.

Lucius was a very attractive man and, though I had eyes only for Bo, it was still disarming to see him in such a state, especially when he was still wearing the pleasure of the hunt so blatantly. His body was strong and stiff from head to toe and everywhere in between.

"Then let's go," he said, breezing past me.

I followed Lucius back to his cabin, all the while trying to look anywhere except at his nude back side. When we reached the steps that led to his front porch, I stopped.

"Why don't you go in and get dressed? You can come and get me when you're done."

Lucius laughed uproariously, a fact that irritated me and further stung my cheeks.

"Oh, to see your face right now, lass, is...well, it's priceless. You're like an innocent angel."

"Alright, alright. Go put some clothes on already," I snapped.

I could hear Lucius chuckling long after he'd closed the door behind him.

Less than a minute later, he re-emerged. Little had changed. His wide, blood-spattered chest was still bear and his dark red hair still hung loose, floating wildly around his face. His feet were bear, but at least now he had on a pair of faded jeans, though they were only zipped, not buttoned.

"What?" he asked, indignation evident in his tone. "I covered all the embarrassing parts, love. Now, why don't we put aside your ridiculous sensibilities and go inside."

When put like that, I felt like a prude. So, with a sigh and a roll of my eyes, I climbed the steps and made my way into the cabin.

Rather than going to the more luxurious quarters below ground, Lucius veered toward the small above-ground kitchen.

"So, I think I ran into some friends of yours," he said amicably, rooting around in a cabinet to bring out a glass.

"What? Where?"

"Just through the trees and beyond the gorge."

I watched as Lucius poured Mountain Dew into the glass.

"When?"

"Oh, not even an hour ago."

A pang of apprehension twitched in my chest.

"Did- did you speak to them or…"

Lucius turned and walked toward me, smiling and holding out the glass. "You mean did I sample them for dessert?"

The teasing gleam in his emerald eyes assured me that he did not, but I still chastised myself for pushing his violent nature to the back of my mind. It could be a fatal mistake to ever let myself forget that Lucius was first and foremost a vampire.

Automatically, I took the proffered glass. "No, that's not what I—"

"Of course that's what you meant, but never fear, lovely Ridley. I shan't snack on your friends."

"Th-thank you."

What else could I say?

"It's really not advisable for them to be traipsing around in the woods, however. You know that."

Lucius walked to the puffy brown couch that faced the fireplace in the living room and sat down in one corner, crossing his legs and facing me.

I thought of Summer's brazen stupidity and I wanted to growl. "I know and, trust me, I tried to talk them out of it. They're just...idiots."

"Ah, careless youth," Lucius said, his smile distant with reminiscence. "I remember it well."

"It's just that they have no idea what's out there. And now, after everything else that's happened, they could be in serious danger."

In fact, I was feeling guiltier by the second for not trying harder to get Summer to change her mind. Of course, by the time I'd been attacked, word had gotten out to the entire school about the party and there would've been no stopping it anyway, but still...

The lilt of a fading Irish brogue broke into my thoughts.

"Sit, lass, and tell me what's on your mind."

I took the seat on the couch opposite Lucius and sipped my Mountain Dew while I decided where to begin. Lucius soon took the initiative and decided for me.

"Has Bo made contact with you?"

Though it was impossible for Lucius to know about our passionate interlude, but still I felt my cheeks burn.

"Yes. He's alive, as you suspected."

Lucius nodded in satisfaction, a pleased grin turning up the corners of his mouth.

"Excellent news."

"I went to visit Denise, Bo's mother," I blurted.

Lucius raised one auburn brow. "And?"

"I think you were right. About the mind control, I mean. It's like she was struggling to reconcile her fading memories with her life before...well, before Bo. It was actually kind of sad," I admitted, my heart aching for the myriad of confusing emotions Denise had suffered at the whim of a vicious vampire.

"Well, when the effects are completely eradicated from her system, she'll be good as new."

I looked at Lucius, trying to tell whether he was telling the truth or just telling me what I wanted to hear. I couldn't determine which it was.

"I hope so," I said absently. Then I remembered the other person that had been there. "I think she's going to take care of it before it has a chance to wear off by itself anyway."

"Who?"

"Heather."

"Heather?"

"Well, I assume that's who has been doing this to Bo's mom. I mean, the morning I was there, I had thought someone else was there with Denise, but I wasn't sure until I went back a few minutes later. I could hear two women talking and when Denise came to the door, she was totally different, like something had happened in the short time I'd been away. She had no idea who I was. It was really weird."

"So you heard another woman's voice?"

"Yep. And I could smell something sweet and floral, distinctly feminine, when she opened the door that second time."

"Hmm," Lucius said, his brow wrinkled in concern.

"Don't you think it was probably Heather?"

"It's possible," he answered noncommittally.

"Well, who else would it be?"

"That's a good question."

I frowned, too. Sometimes, Lucius talked in circles. Sometimes, I doubted his forthrightness. Sometimes, I got the feeling he was playing for another side in the game. Not necessarily the bad side, but just not our side.

"That aside, do you still think that Bo is the boy who can't be killed?"

"Well, that seems to further the theory, now doesn't it?"

"It seems to," I said coyly. Clearing my throat, I asked, "So, what else do you know about that legend? I mean, in case it is Bo."

"The boy was supposedly the son of two angels, a child who God Himself empowered to kill his father. Some legends say his father was Constantine and that he was the very first one of us."

"Do you believe that?"

Lucius shrugged. "That particular story doesn't fit because Constantine died many years ago, and according to that legend, the boy would become mortal after the death of his father. Unless, of course, Constantine wasn't his father. But there are many other stories of how it all began that are much more believable than that one anyway. Then again, if Bo can't be killed..."

Lucius cast me an odd sidelong look that brought the hairs on my arms to attention. I got the feeling that he was hiding something from me, but I wasn't quite sure how to root it out. Of course, I could always just ask.

I took a deep breath. "There's something you're not telling me. What is it, Lucius? What are you not telling me?"

Piercing green eyes bored holes into mine, but I didn't look away. I wasn't going to back down. Good or bad, I wanted to know. I needed to know.

"There is a legend- well, actually, it's part of the same legend about the boy who can't be killed."

Lucius paused, looking down into his lap and fiddling with the seam in his jeans, driving me crazy with curiosity, making me wait.

"And?" I prompted sharply after at least one full minute had passed.

"It speaks of God's punishment to the angel who defied Him for love, the father of the boy who can't be killed. Legend says that this angel will ultimately be killed by love. It tells of a girl, the one true mate of the boy who can't be killed. Supposedly, this girl would provide him with the means by which to kill his father, fulfilling his destiny and regaining his mortality."

My whole being was focused on what he was saying, on the implications. I felt hyper alert and twitchy. I felt like my entire future was riding on his words. I don't know why, but I did.

"How? How will she do that?"

Lucius finally looked up and met my eyes again.

"It is said that God wrote it on her very skin and that only the boy would be able to understand it, to decipher it."

I felt the blood seep from my cheeks.

"Oh," I said, my shoulders slumping forward in dejection.

I felt deflated. No, I felt crushed. For just a moment, I had experienced a rush of...something—pleasure, fate, inevitability—at the prospect of being destined for Bo, of being the one person in the history of the world that could help him. But there was nothing on my skin. I washed it and clothed it every day; I knew it intimately. There was simply nothing there.

"Well, if that legend is true, then I must not be Bo's mate," I said quietly.

Speaking those hurtful words aloud nearly brought me to tears. I looked down into the glass of bright yellow liquid, blinking away the moisture that had suddenly accumulated behind my lids.

"I guess that depends on how you look at it."

"That sounds pretty clear to me. I think the girl would know, don't you?"

Lucius merely shrugged again, watching me closely. Is that what he was trying to tell me? That there was someone else?

The mere thought of another girl being divinely mated to Bo made my stomach swim with nausea. The air inside the tiny cabin suddenly felt too warm and too thick to breathe, so I jumped to my feet and made my excuses. I had to get out of there.

"Well, I'd better get going," I said, handing Lucius my still-full glass of soda. "I need to go and try to get my friends out of the woods. I'd hate for them to be attacked, too."

I walked toward the door, willing myself not to run—from Lucius, from fate, from the loss of Bo. Again.

"Too?" Lucius asked from behind me.

When I turned to look back, his face was only inches from mine. I hadn't even heard him get up or make his way across the wooden floor to me. He was just...there. That was always a bit unnerving.

"Pardon?" He'd startled me, addling my already scrambled brain, a feat not particularly difficult by that point.

"You said you'd hate for them to be attacked 'too'."

"Oh, right."

I'd completely forgotten to mention being attacked in my bedroom by a female vampire.

"Well?" It was Lucius doing the prompting now.

I shrugged, not wanting to make a big deal out of it, even though it still felt like a big deal. I just wanted to get out of there.

"Some vampire came into my room and attacked me."

His jewel-like gaze hardened, focusing on my face with surprising intensity.

"When did this happen?"

"The other night."

"What did he look like? Did you recognize him?"

"No, I couldn't see anything, but I think it was a 'her' not a 'him'."

Lucius's nostrils flared, as if he was attempting to smell something on me—or in me.

"Lucius, I've gotta go," I said, hurrying out the door and down the steps. As I walked, I dragged gasps of cool air into my lungs, determined to hold back the despair that threatened.

The legend is wrong. It's wrong. It's got to be wrong, I kept telling myself as I came to a stop just inside the tree line.

"Do you even know where you're going?" Lucius called to me from the front porch.

I started walking again, tossing back over my shoulder. "Which way?" I had to ask; I had no idea in which direction the gorge lay.

"When you get to the boulder, go right and keep straight. You can't miss the glow of the fire in the distance," he called.

His voice had grown faint as I increased the distance between us, increased the distance between me and the nagging pain of the truth, or what might be the truth. I wouldn't, couldn't let myself believe it just yet.

As I navigated the darkened trees and treacherous forest floor, I found I could no longer hold the devastation I felt inside. Pain bubbled up from deep in my soul and poured down my cheeks in the form of tears. They flowed in tortured silence, dripping from my chin and peppering my chest with salt water.

I don't know how long I walked like that. Time ceased to move around me. I was trapped in a web of despair and I couldn't see my way out.

When I saw the orangey halo of the fire bleeding out into the night, I stopped behind a tree, leaning up against it and wiping at my face, trying to collect myself before I walked on to crash a party.

As soon as I felt mostly composed, I walked casually up to two people I recognized that were standing at the periphery of the gathering.

"Hey, guys. Having fun?"

Mike Eversol and Shaina Dunn turned to look at me.

"Ridley," Shaina said, leaning forward to hug me. "I thought you weren't coming."

I shrugged. "I'm just dropping by. I can't stay very long." I scanned the faces in the crowd, but didn't see Summer. "Do you know where Summer is?"

Shaina turned to look out into the crowd as well. "Um, I thought she was over at the keg with Aisha, but I don't see her now. I don't know where she went." She turned back to me. "Sorry."

I smiled. "No biggee. I'm sure she's here somewhere. I'll just ask around," I explained, backing away.

"See you later," she said.

"Later, Ridley," Mike chimed in.

I waved then turned to wiggle my way through the tight throng of bodies and weave my way around the fire until I'd arrived at the keg. There was no sign of Summer or Aisha.

I spotted Drew. As usual, he was never far from the source of alcohol. He was laughing at something Minty was saying, but when he spotted me, his smile faded.

If he hadn't seen me, I'd have done my best to just avoid him. But, since that option was off the table and there was no polite way to not speak, I approached the duo nonchalantly and asked, "Hey, have you guys seen Summer?"

"Yeah, she—" Minty began, but Drew interrupted him.

"You here alone?"

"Yep."

"Can't get a date since wonder boy disappeared, huh?"

Bitterness radiated from him like cold air from an open freezer door. Drew was not so callous that he didn't care that Bo had "disappeared," nor would he maliciously wish for someone to be hurt or harmed; he was simply still sore from being dumped.

Men and their egos! I thought.

"Nope. Where's Summer?" I asked again, ignoring his comment and refusing to take the bait.

With a snort, Drew turned his head and took a long pull from his cup, one presumably full of beer.

Minty, having been watching our exchange with visible discomfort, answered me when Drew didn't.

"I saw her and Aisha walking off into the woods. I think they were going to use the bathroom. You know how girls are," he said, rolling his eyes. "Two by two."

I grinned. "You mean smart for not going off into the woods alone?"

"Touché, Heller," Minty teased.

"Which way did they go?"

"Back that way," he said, pointing behind us, into the darkest part of the woods, the part furthest from the fire.

Figures!

"Ok. Thanks, Minty."

I walked off, not even deigning to acknowledge Drew. I wasn't going to waste my time on him until he grew up and got over himself.

When I'd gotten into the trees and far enough away from the party to hear the night, I stopped to listen. Wherever Summer and Aisha were, their chatter would lead me to them.

As I listened, however, I realized that there was one problem with that—there was no chatter. There were no noises that might suggest that anyone besides me was in the woods away from the others.

Even while I was thinking how odd that was, foreboding was swelling ominously inside my head like a big thunderhead.

Swallowing the unease that rose to the back of my throat, I walked further into the darkness and stopped once more to listen. Nothing.

"Summer!" I called, not too loudly.

Nothing.

"Aisha!"

Nothing.

"Summer!" I shouted more loudly this time, walking a few steps farther into the night.

Still, I heard nothing but the leaves and bracken settling beneath my feet.

Just before I turned to head back to the party, a burst of wind puffed my hair away from my face. It was as if something had passed in front of me, moving so quickly that I couldn't see it.

I held my breath and listened. The faint whispers of cloth shifting against skin reached my ears. I looked left then right, but saw nothing in the blackness.

"Summer?"

I turned in a circle, all my senses reaching out to scan my surroundings for someone, for something. When I was again staring into the dimmest part of the woods, that rush of wind feathered across my face again, only this time, it carried the scent of earth, as well as a sound.

"T," the soft voice sighed.

Fear needled at my nerves. The voice was so low I couldn't make out anything familiar in it, but that letter, that nickname, was one that Drew used to call me.

Adrenaline flooded my body, infusing my muscles and my heart with blood and oxygen, preparing me for flight. In one smooth movement, I turned on my heel and I ran as fast as I could back toward the light of the bonfire.

I didn't have to see behind to know that something was following me. Closely. That knowledge, that feeling like I was prey, pushed me faster and faster through the forest.

Just before I burst through the trees into the clearing where the party was happening, something hit me in the back. I screamed as the skin between my shoulder blades tore beneath the scrape of something razor sharp.

I practically fell into the arms of one very surprised Minty.

"What the h—"

"Minty, run!"

"Ridley, what the—"

"Run!" I yelled at the top of my lungs. I moved away from Minty to approach the fire. "Run!" I repeated.

"Ridley, your back," Minty said from behind me.

I turned toward him and that's when I heard the frightened screams erupt from several girls that were standing around.

"What?" I asked, twisting my arm to reach behind me. When I drew my fingers away, they were bloody.

I looked up at Minty. He was staring at my sticky red hand.

"Minty, we've got to get everyone out of the woods."

It wasn't hard to convince the already-scared girls to stick together and get the heck out of dodge, and I found that the more reluctant partiers were easier to motivate once I showed them my back. I saw Minty pointing to me a couple of times and realized that he was using the same tactic. No one wanted to be shredded for the sake of a party.

When everyone was heading quickly back to the road, to their cars, Minty crossed behind the fire, over to me.

"Let's go, Ridley. We need to get you to the hospital."

"Where's Drew?"

Minty paled visibly. "He- he—"

"He what?"

"He went to take a leak right after you left."

Minty was afraid Drew might be in danger. After learning that Drew had disappeared into the woods shortly after I had, I was even more afraid that Drew might be the danger.

"Minty, we've got to get out of here."

"I can't leave—"

"Minty, there's nothing we can do for him now. We'll never find him in the dark."

I saw the indecision on Minty's face as he warred between self-preservation and loyalty to his friend.

"Minty, he wouldn't want you to die looking for him."

I hated to be the one encouraging someone else to leave a friend behind, but Minty had no idea what Drew might have become, what he could be capable of. And unfortunately, he would never know that I wasn't intentionally sacrificing Drew's life for his, that I wasn't a coward. He would just have to think poorly of me. It was the only way.

Finally, after a few more seconds of hesitation, Minty nodded and we quickly hurried after the crowd.

As we walked, neither of us said a word. We were both lost in thought, though I doubted the same thoughts. He was feeling guilty for leaving his friend, yet afraid for his own safety. I was wondering how in the world I could've missed that Drew was a vampire.

CHAPTER FIVE

It took some fancy talking to get Minty to forego taking me to the hospital himself. I knew he felt indebted to me, like I'd saved his life and he needed to return the favor. But I finally got him to see that I would get into huge trouble if I left my car abandoned by the side of the road.

Reluctantly, he dropped me off at my Civic. He wanted to follow me to the hospital, but I deterred him, telling him he needed to make sure that as many people as he could find got out of the woods without harm. I could tell by the determined look on his face that he would take that mission seriously. I almost expected him to salute me or say "Aye, aye, Cap'n."

Once I was alone, I hopped in the car, jerked out my cell and started speed dialing. I tried Summer's phone and got no answer. I tried Aisha's phone and got no answer. Then I tried them both again. And again. And again.

When it became glaringly obvious that redial wasn't going to magically make them pick up the phone, I started the car and headed home. On the way, more than ever, I wished that I had some way of reaching Bo. I had questions, concerns, doubts. I needed to feel that amazing buzz of his closeness, to let it drown out everything but Bo and the overwhelming feelings that I had for him.

I drove to the house, hoping that Mom and Dad would be asleep. And, much to my relief, they were. Dad would be tired from his flight and Mom would be fighting an addiction. Both led very fatiguing lives, but in two totally different ways.

****

The next morning I woke with my cell phone plastered to my face where I'd slept on it. I'd apparently fallen asleep between my every-ten-minute calls to Summer and Aisha. At least I'd gotten hold of Minty, though. He'd spoken to nearly everyone he'd seen at the party and they were all fine. Except Summer, Aisha and Drew of course.

He'd asked if I'd gone to the hospital. I didn't want to lie, so I told him that I'd come home and that my injury wasn't as bad as we'd thought, certainly nothing worthy of a trip to the ER.

And that was the truth. As soon as I'd crept past my parents, I'd gone straight to my bathroom to assess the damage. My sweater was shredded, but my skin, though deeply scratched in four long gashes, wasn't as bad as I'd expected. In fact, it looked to have already begun healing. It didn't even bother my sleep (obviously, since I'd slept with a phone as my pillow).

Before I sat up in the bed, I sniffed. For the first time in weeks, I couldn't smell Bo. I could only assume he hadn't visited me, though I shouldn't have been surprised. Since my unwanted female vampire visitor, I'd been keeping my window closed. Unfortunately, that barred Bo from entry as well, unless of course he wanted to break it, which he would only do if I was in imminent danger.

Unbidden, Lucius's story popped into my head. I couldn't help but wonder if he'd found that mate that was somewhere out there, waiting to rescue him. With a growl in my throat and an ache in my chest, I pushed that thought aside and dialed Summer for the zillionth time.

Still no answer. Same with Aisha. I wasn't going to call Drew, of course. I'd be avoiding him like the plague in the future.

I was lying in bed, debating on how best to spend my day when my phone chirped. I nearly dropped it in my haste to answer. I didn't even check the caller ID; I just hit the button and said hello.

"Ridley, the nicest, sweetest, prettiest girl in the whole school. How are you, my friend?"

It was Savannah on the other end of the line, laying it on thick. That could only mean one thing.

"Uh-oh. What are you getting ready to ask me to do?"

Her last idea had involved breaking into the marina, stealing a boat and launching a lantern out onto the water to honor her dead mother, a felony that never happened because we were accosted by vampires en route.

"Oh, come on. It's nothing that bad."

"That bad?"

"Well, I don't think it's bad at all."

I sighed. "Alright, spill. What is it?"

"I want you to go with me to the Halloween dance tonight. Since we are both, like, almost widows, I think we should go together. I think it would be fun, and we both need to get out and do something carefree."

I couldn't argue that point. I needed some fun. And some "carefree." I could barely remember what that felt like. Anymore, my life was consumed with an aching need and an ever-growing hole in my heart. And sprinkled between those two were spots of fear and depression, frustration and loneliness. My life had been no picnic since I'd met Bo. But I wouldn't have it any other way. I couldn't even think of giving him up.

As if on cue, my chest squeezed at the haunting prospect of losing him to someone he couldn't deny, someone he'd be bound to in a way that he'd never be bound to me.

Like I'd done a hundred times already, I refused to let my mind travel that path. Instead, I did the unthinkable. I agreed to go with Savannah.

"I'll go. You're right, we need some fun."

"Really? You will?" Savannah squealed.

I couldn't help but smile as I held the phone at arm's length. "Yes, but I'd like to have some small amount of hearing left so that I can enjoy the music," I teased.

"Oh, sorry. I just figured you'd say no."

"Why?"

"I don't know. Sometimes you look so sad when I see you. I thought maybe I remind you of Bo," she confessed soberly.

I hated that she saw me that way. I hated that she thought that. I hated that my misery without Bo was so perceptible.

"No, you don't. And, who knows? Maybe you'll see a whole different Ridley tonight."

"R-eally? 'Cause you know I can't see a thing, right?"

Even though it was simply Savannah's way, to make fun of her infirmity, I still felt the heat rush to my cheeks. It made me feel wretched when she did.

"Then maybe I'll have to do something fun that you can hear. How 'bout that?"

"Ooo, like what? Burp the alphabet? Fart The Star Spangled Banner?"

That actually coaxed a laugh out of me. "You're insane, you know that?"

"Oh, come on. You wouldn't have me any other way."

"You're right, I wouldn't."

"Ok, so pick me up at eight? Or do you want me to drive?"

"No! No, I'll take care of the driving. You just worry about getting dressed. Don't be wearin' a Bride of Frankenstein head with a Smurf body."

"Listen to Ridley, finally catching on."

"Ha ha."

"Seriously," Savannah said, her voice turning solemn. "I don't want anyone to see me differently, to treat me differently. I can make fun of myself because it's healthier than letting it eat away at me. So I do."

"I know, Savannah. It just feels…wrong."

"Well, I guess you're just going to have to get over that."

With an exaggerated sigh, I agreed. "Yep, I guess I will."

"Alrighty then, eight o'clock?"

"Eight o'clock."

"Ciao."

And with that, she hung up in her abrupt, very Savannah-like manner. I had to admit, though, that she'd brightened my day. How pathetic is that, when your mood is so dark that someone who's just lost her sight and her boyfriend ends up being the cheerful one?

With a renewed zeal for getting out of bed, I pushed back the covers and walked to my closet. I had no idea what to wear to a Halloween costume party. It was the first one the school had ever had. I didn't think it really mattered, though. It wasn't the party I was looking forward to as much as spending time with Savannah. It seemed she was just what I needed—a friend and a distraction.

I pulled out a couple of possibilities and laid them on the bed and then made my way to the kitchen. It was Saturday and Dad was home. That meant only one thing: time to brush off my daytime Emmy and get to work pretending.

Mom was standing in front of the coffee maker. Her back was to me and both hands were flat on the counter, her shoulders hunched as if she was in pain.

"Mom?" I said, rushing to her side. "What's wrong?"

I leaned around to look into her face. I was relieved to see that there were no tears. No tears meant that whatever was ailing her was fixable.

Haunted, bloodshot eyes met mine. "Your father went to get breakfast. I'm just having some coffee. Why don't you pour yourself some juice?"

With that, she straightened, her eyes falling to the mug that sat on the counter in front of her. She reached for it with a hand that shook so badly she nearly spilled the hot brew just trying to pick it up.

"Here," I said, wrapping my fingers around the handle. "Why don't you come over here and sit down. I'll get the drinks ready and set the table."

I carried Mom's coffee mug for her. When she sat down, she put her elbows on the table and I handed her the cup. Her shaking wasn't nearly as perceptible with the support of the table under her arms.

She closed her eyes as she took a sip of the steaming liquid. When she opened them, they locked on mine. A small smile tugged at the corners of her mouth. It wasn't much as far as expressions go, but there was a lot more gratitude in her eyes. Once again, I had helped her avert disaster. She knew it and I knew it. She was my mother, though, and I loved her. She knew her secret was safe with me. After all, a family of pretenders had to stick together.

We made it through breakfast. And lunch. And dinner. I knew better than to make too many other plans for the weekend days when Dad was home. He was adamant about spending "quality family time" together. It was a farce, but he was a stickler about it.

With the last of the dinner dishes tucked safely away inside the dishwasher, I closed it and hit the start button. I was on my way back to my room to shower when I remembered something.

I returned to the living room.

"Mom, do you still have that mask that you wore to the masquerade party you guys went to year before last? The silver one?"

I could see Mom struggling to remember. I'm sure it was like trying to flip through the pages of a soggy newspaper.

"Gosh, Ridley, that's been a while. Why don't you check the box in the top of my closet. If I kept it, it would probably be in there."

"Ok. Thanks."

I headed straight for her room and got the box down. Sure enough, the mask was in there. Intact, too. Luckily, it only covered the top portion of the face, so there was virtually no chance it might have puke on it. Sadly, that was a constant consideration when borrowing anything of Mom's that didn't predate Izzy's death.

After my shower and an intense buffing session, I smoothed on some shimmering lotion and let it dry before slipping into a dress that I'd worn in a beauty pageant a couple years prior. Though it was snug, it still fit, and the tight factor only enhanced the look I was going for.

The dress had a white bodice that hugged me in a corset style. The lower half was fitted and covered in silver sequins. The very bottom of the dress flared out and had layers and layers of white frothy material spilling from beneath the sequins, making it look like a tail. It was a curve-hugging mermaid dress if I'd ever seen one.

I left my hair long, flowing in thick waves down my back. Once I had my makeup on, I sprayed some perfume behind my ears and in my cleavage and then put on the mask. With its silver, white and blue sequins, laid out in a design that curled and swirled around my eyes and over my forehead, I thought I looked the part: a mysterious sea siren.

A little pang of longing and loneliness pinched at my insides. It would be perfect if I was going to the dance with Bo, a magical night to match my magical costume.

I shook off the melancholy direction my thoughts were taking me. Tonight, I refused to mope. For one night, I was going to do my best to pretend that I was a normal teen going to a dance to have a little fun. No drama, no sadness, no soul-mate issues. Just fun. Carefree fun. Plain and simple.

I slipped on my shoes, said my goodbyes and headed for the car. As my hair shifted against my back, I noticed there wasn't even so much as a prickle of pain where my scratches were. I reached back and felt beneath my hair. The skin was smooth, despite the fact that I hadn't really focused on my back with my scrubbing and lotion application. The scratches were gone without a trace.

When I got to Savannah's I walked in tiny steps to the door and knocked. Her dad answered, letting me inside to await Savannah.

"You look very pretty, Ridley," he said kindly.

"Thank you, Mr. Grant."

"Call me Jeremy," he insisted. "Mermaid?" he asked nodding to my dress.

"Yes, sir," I said, smiling.

Good. At least there was no question about what I was made up to be. If nothing else, I wanted my costume to be a clear departure from the normal "everything gone slutty" attire that many females chose to sport on Halloween.

"Would you like something to drink while you wait? I've got Dr. Pepper, orange juice, Propel and—"

Mr. Grant's voice trailed off when movement drew his eye down the hallway behind me. I turned to look in that direction as well.

Savannah was making her way slowly toward us. She looked amazing. How a blind girl accomplished what she had was beyond me.

She was wearing a black dress that looked slick and scaly and it fit her perfectly. She had silver rattles at her wrists and ankles, and she wore silver sunglasses to hide her eyes. Her plump lips were stained blood red and her skin was porcelain smooth.

But it was her hair that told the real story. She had curled her already-wavy mess of red locks and then I assumed used hairspray to define each thick wiggling strand and make it stand away from her scalp. If I'd only been able to see her head, I'd still have known who she was—Medusa.

"You look awesome!" And I meant it. She did.

"Vanna, you look beautiful," Mr. Grant said, awe evident in his voice. "You look so much like your mother."

A sadness that was becoming all too familiar to me lit his eyes when he walked to Savannah and reached out to touch her cheek. In the likeness of his daughter, he was seeing the love of his life, living and breathing again, right in front of him. I knew by the pain in his eyes that he would mourn the loss of her forever.

As I watched him adore his daughter, knowledge slammed into my gut like a steel fist, knowledge that someday—maybe even someday soon—I would lose Bo. Again. Only this time, for real. Forever. I wouldn't lose him to death. Never to death. I would lose him to another love, a love I couldn't compete with. And then I, too, would spend the rest of my life mourning him, the love I loved the most.

"Alright, Dad. Don't get all creepy and ooey-gooey," Savannah teased.

When Savannah took off her sunglasses and started fiddling with them, I thought at first that it was a nervous gesture. But then, when she looked up and I saw her eyes, I knew that it wasn't. The sadness of her father was reflected in the warm brown pools, and I felt guilty for forgetting that Savannah knew all about loss, too.

"Sorry, honey," he said, plastering a brave smile on his handsome face. "You girls have fun tonight. Just not too much. Stay away from shirtless boys with a six pack and tight pants," he warned.

"Right, Dad. Way to make things less weird."

I couldn't help but grin at their exchange. Their life together, while tragic, was like a reprieve in a way. And their light banter helped to diffuse the desperate sadness that had swallowed up all the air in the room.

Savannah turned and walked cautiously to the door. I followed. So did Mr. Grant.

He opened the door and held it while we exited. "Home by midnight."

Savannah sighed. "Fine, Mr. Cleaver. Midnight."

Mr. Grant smiled tolerantly, shaking his head in exasperation.

I was uncertain what I should do to help Savannah, but she took the reins and reached out to grab hold of my forearm.

"Just gonna leave a blind girl to trip and fall, is that it?"

I laughed nervously. Her teasing took some getting used to.

"I'm kidding, Ridley. Just let me hold your arm and don't get too far ahead of me. We'll be fine."

She said it so tenderly, so compassionately, as if she knew that I was struggling with my role in the night, with my role as her friend. I just wanted to hug her. Beneath all her joking, wise-cracking and goof-balling, Savannah was really pretty amazing. Devon had seen it first. It had taken the rest of us a little longer to catch on.

Once she was seated in the car, I shut the door and started to walk off. Her shriek stopped me.

"What?" I said, jerking open the door. "What is it?"

"You shut the door on my tail," she said in a forlorn voice.

It was just then that I saw that her dress tapered off in the back to a long, narrow train that looked like an elegant tail, perfect for Medusa's lower snaky half.

Savannah picked up the material and placed it gently in her lap, sniffling delicately.

"My tail! It's broken."

I know my face must've been comically horrified. Until I heard her laughing.

"You're mean as the snake you're wearing," I said, slamming the door shut and walking around to the driver's side.

"Gotcha 'gin," she boasted happily.

"Are you always like this?"

She pursed her lips for just a minute, while she thought. "Yeah, pretty much."

"How does your dad stand it?"

"He laughs a lot."

"I bet," I said, starting the engine and shifting into gear.

Once we'd arrived at the school, there was practically a party around Savannah, our new school celebrity. She handled the spotlight with admirable aplomb, however, and I just stood back and watched her.

I searched the costumes for something that seemed like a Summer look or an Aisha style, but I saw neither of them, nor did I see Drew.

Maybe they're not here yet, I thought. Or maybe they're disguised better than what you'd think, like as angels or something equally dichotomous.

To get my mind off them, I surveyed the gym. It was decorated with all sorts of macabre materials and paraphernalia. Tons of spider web loaded with spiders and bloody fingers and severed limbs hung above the dance floor. Black lights stood in all four corners, making the black seem blacker and the white seem to glow. There was a refreshments table set against one wall with a faux stone path that led to it. It wandered through headstones and fog, like you might find in a real cemetery—minus the zombie heads-and-hands emerging from the haze, of course.

I admired it all as the cheerfully costumed students continued to clamor around Savannah.

The loud music faded into the familiar thump of a not-quite-slow song. Its beat brought to mind steamy nights and writhing bodies. The sensual rhythm called to many of the people surrounding Savannah, beckoning them to the dance floor. Scary couples and gruesome groups started to move in unison to the heavy bass. I searched the made-up and masked faces for Savannah until I located her bright, serpentine halo. She'd been lassoed into a dance by a dead cowboy I recognized. He sat three rows behind me in study hall.

Suddenly aware of being the lone person not on the dance floor dancing, I turned to make my way around to the refreshments table. I was skirting the writhing mob of dancers when I felt a familiar tug in my belly.

I stopped in my tracks and looked around. Immediately, my heart sped up, banging like a drum, keeping time with the erratic expansion of my lungs as I grew more and more breathless.

I searched the faces for the one that occupied far too many of my thoughts, but I didn't see him. I could've almost convinced myself that I'd been mistaken, but the magnetism that I felt intensified with every breath, assuring me that it was no mistake. Those invisible strings were pulling me, no dragging me into the middle of the crowd, where bodies were crushed together so tightly they moved as if they were one.

Weaving my way through perfumed and cologned figures, I felt like I was getting lost in the fray when I saw a tall, darkly cloaked figure watching me through a break in the mob.

He was dressed as Dracula. His robe was ebony satin with a blood red lining and the hood that covered his head shadowed all but his mouth.

My breath hitched in my throat and burned in my lungs. My pulse thumped wildly and my skin tingled in response to a presence that I couldn't forget. It was Bo. Beneath the hood that concealed most of his face and the cloak that concealed most of his body, I knew it was him. I'd know him anywhere. I'd love him always.

I could see only his handsomely square jaw and chiseled mouth. My eyes hungrily memorized the lips that I'd never forget the taste of. I felt like I'd been starved of them for far too long.

As Bo's hand rose slowly from his side, reaching out to me through the crowd of bodies, the words to the song carved themselves onto my heart. Bo was both my sweetest dream and my most beautiful nightmare.

Without hesitation, I stepped forward and slipped my hand into his. A little bolt of electricity shot up my arm when our skin made contact. Bo pulled me to him and I inhaled, reveling in the tangy scent that had teased me for what seemed like forever, and probably always would.

Bodies brushed me from every angle, every direction, but the only thing that I felt was Bo pressed to my front from chest to thigh. I looked up into the most consuming eyes I'd ever seen and I fell into them, sinking into the only place I ever really wanted to be.

I saw Bo's lips move and, even above the music, I heard his whisper.

"I never thought I'd get to love someone so beautiful," he said.

The words echoed through my soul and warmed me to my toes. With Bo staring down at me, his words in my ears, his body moving gently against mine, it was the most surreal moment—dream-like, so much so I never wanted to wake from it.

The music surrounded us, wrapping us in a pulsing cocoon of privacy amid the sea of bodies. I laid my palms flat against Bo's chest as one of his hands snaked around my waist. The fingers of his other hand teased the skin of my arm as they made their way up to disappear beneath the hair at my nape. I felt them tangle in my hair and then curl into a light fist.

With one quick tug, Bo pulled my head to the side as he bent toward me.

I gasped when I felt his hot lips at my throat. I pressed my body closer to his, running my hands down the sides of his firm abdomen. I felt the hard muscles contract beneath my fingertips as Bo's breath hissed through his teeth.

Lyrics about guilty pleasure wove a sensual web around us. My blood heated with thoughts of Bo's skin on mine, covering me, sliding against me.

The friction of Bo's body rubbing against mine, moving in time with the music, sang along my nerves and turned my core into a raging inferno. When I felt his tongue licking at the pulse that beat violently beneath my ear, I had to bite my lip to keep a moan from escaping.

"There's no one like you," he said, his lips tickling my sensitive skin as he spoke. "There's no taste like you," he sighed, trailing his tongue up to tease the lobe of my ear, drawing it gently into his mouth. "No feel like you," he moaned, his hand moving to the base of my spine and pressing my hips into his. "There's no one that I need like I need you."

My insides melted. I wanted to cry with the pleasure of it, the bitter-sweetness of it. I couldn't imagine ever wanting someone as much as I wanted Bo. I didn't think my heart could take it without exploding. I would gladly give up years of my life to be with him, if only for a little while. In the end, I knew it would be worth it.

Bo raised his head to look at me, his eyes searing me with a heat so intense, I felt it in my stomach. Without a word, he tightened his hold on me and lifted until my feet were several inches from the ground and my chest was plastered to his. Slowly, he turned and walked out of the crush, away from the crowd.

He carried me toward a deserted corner of the gymnasium and into a short, dark hallway that led to a door that emptied out onto the stage in the auditorium right next door.

The music still thudded in my chest, obscuring the excited patter of my heart. Bo walked to the back of the hallway, to its blackest point, and stopped, pushing me up against the wall and holding me there with his body. And then his mouth was devouring mine.

As his tongue tangled mercilessly with mine, I grabbed his shoulders and held on tight. I felt his hands at my thighs, his fingers working the material of my dress up until I could feel skin on skin.

I wanted Bo so badly it almost hurt. I wanted more. I wanted it all and the frustration of it was killing me.

At first, the scream sounded like it came from somewhere inside me, like the cry of my body for Bo's attention suddenly became audible. But then I heard the music die and an uncharacteristic hush fall across the gymnasium, which lay only a few feet away.

Bo leaned back and looked at me, both of us breathing like we'd just run a marathon. Confusion and a little concern swirled in his beautiful, velvety eyes. A frown creased his shadowed brow as he let me slide to the floor. My dress shimmied down my legs and righted itself at my ankles as we both turned to look toward the gym.

Bo took my hand and led me from the dark, back out to where everyone was shuffling to get a better view of something that was happening around the refreshments table, near the exit.

The closer we got, I could hear that someone was crying. A girl. And one of the chaperones was soothing her, encouraging her to calm down and tell him what happened.

Bo and I pushed our way to the far right interior edge of the crowd so we could see. It was Bailey Adams. She was dressed as a cat in a skin-tight black suit. The material was torn down her arm, her tail was missing and one of her ears was bent. A fine red spatter covered her face—blood. She'd obviously rubbed at it, causing it to streak across her cheek and smear her whiskers.

She was hiccupping, bawling her eyes out, trying to speak around her terror.

"Take your time, Bailey. Just tell me what happened. Are you hurt?"

"No. She didn't want me. She took Jason."

"Who? Who took Jason?"

"Summer. She took him."

"Summer? Summer Collins?"

"Yes," Bailey cried, her sobbing renewed. "I think that's who it was. She jumped out from behind the side of the school and attacked us. We both fell down to the ground, but it was him she wanted. She started biting him. She took two big chunks out of his face. Right in front of me. I-I-I saw her do it," she stammered hysterically.

"I crawled over to him and grabbed his arm, tried to pull him away from her, but she wouldn't let him go. She just chewed on him and kind of shook him, like a-like a- a toy. Blood was going everywhere and- and then she got up, grabbed hold of his foot and dragged him off."

Mr. Hall looked suspicious. "Bailey, are you sure that's what you saw?"

"Uh-huh," she said solemnly, nodding her head and wiping the tears from her eyes with the back of her hand.

"Summer Collins? Attacked Jason and…and…"

"Dragged him off," she supplied.

"Dragged him off?"

"Right."

"Could it have been a prank, Bailey? Are you sure what you saw was real?"

Onlookers started murmuring, looking at one another. A prank like that would be epic. But Summer? That just didn't sound like her at all. Not the Summer I knew anyway. Of course, I hadn't seen that Summer, the one I did know, in a while.

"Ok," Mr. Hall sighed, resigned. "Let me call the police and then I'll call your parents, alright?"

Bailey nodded, sniffling, as Mr. Hall pulled out his cell phone and dialed 911.

"I want everyone to stay inside until the police get here," he announced as he waited for someone to come on the line.

Hushed whispers broke out among the masqueraders and the horde started to disburse a bit now that the spectacle was over. Bo took my hand and pulled me away from everyone else.

"Stay here," he said. "I'm going to see if I can find them."

"Do you think Summer's a...a..." I said, looking at him meaningfully.

His brow furrowed. "That's the thing. It doesn't sound like it. A new one of us would've gone straight for the throat, not the face."

"Then what are you thinking?"

"I don't know," he said vaguely. "Just stay here with Savannah. I'll be back."

And then, with a peck on my lips, Bo was gone. Just as quickly and mysteriously as he'd appeared at the dance, he left it. It was at least a full minute before something he'd said finally registered—Savannah.

I'd forgotten all about Savannah.

Frantically, I whirled about, searching the crowd for her vivid hair. I didn't see her anywhere. Fear swelled in my throat like a suffocating balloon.

I started asking everyone I passed, "Have you seen Savannah?" All shook their heads. No one had seen her.

I found the dead cowboy she'd danced with and I asked him. He was marginally more helpful.

"She went to the bathroom right before Bailey came in freaking out. I haven't seen her since."

The knot in my throat grew and my chest squeezed in impending panic.

Ohmigod! Ohmigod! Ohmigod!

I flew from the gym, out the door and down the hall toward the first set of bathrooms I came to. Surely she would've used the closest ones since she was no longer able to see her way around.

Guilt rose up inside me, mingling with the fear, threatening to choke me. What if she'd tried to find me and I was off making out with Bo? What if something had happened to her because I'd been so wrapped up in my own selfish world that I'd completely forgotten about her?

I hit the bathroom door at a run. It slammed back against the wall and rocked on its hinges.

"Savannah! Savannah, are you in here?"

I listened, praying I would hear her delicate voice. When nothing but silence greeted me, I turned to leave. If need be, I'd search every square inch of the school until I found her.

Just as the door was closing behind me, I heard a soft whisper. I caught the door with my foot and whirled back around. I heard the other door, the one on the opposite side of the bathroom that opened onto the back hall, creak as it closed.

"Savannah!" I called again.

"Ridley?"

A relief so profound, so draining washed through me that I thought my legs might fold. I couldn't bear it if something else happened to Savannah, especially on my watch. I felt like I'd already let her down enough by keeping things from her, important things. I couldn't hurt her any more.

"Ohmigod, Savannah, you scared me to death!" I was literally clutching my chest. "Are you alright?"

"I'm fine," she murmured from one of the stalls.

"Where are you?"

"In this one," she said, tapping at the third door with her knuckles.

I walked to stand in front of it. "Can I open the door?"

"Sure."

I pushed the squeaky metal door back and there was Savannah, sitting on top of the closed toilet lid, holding her silver sunglasses between her fingers, smiling like she'd just won a million bucks.

"What are you doing?"

She giggled with delight. "Ridley, I saw him. I saw him!" she exclaimed, her eyes filling with tears. "He's alive."

"Who?"

"Devon."

CHAPTER SIX

My heart tripped over itself for a few beats. "Devon? What? He's alive?"

"Yes!"

"But- but- how do you know?"

"I told you I just saw him."

"You saw him? You mean you talked to him? Tonight? Here?"

"Yes, I talked to him, but Ridley, I saw him."

It had been a very emotionally tumultuous night and I wasn't the quickest at that moment, but I felt inordinately confused by what she was saying.

"What do you mean you 'saw him'?"

She laughed out right this time. "I mean exactly that. I saw him."

I hated to be the one to point out the obvious, but...

"But Savannah, you're blind. You can't see anything."

"You think I don't know that, Ridley? I know I'm blind, but I saw him. I can see him."

Then something scary occurred to me. What if she was hurt? Delusional?

"Savannah, are you hurt? Did you fall in here? Hit your head or something?"

I bent forward and started gently probing her head, checking for cuts or blood. Savannah grabbed my wrists in a firm grip and tugged my hands away from her. I stopped and looked down into her beautiful, sparkling chocolate eyes. They were clear and lucid, though they stared right through me, unseeing.

"Ridley, I'm fine. I'm telling you, I saw Devon."

"But, I don't—"

"I don't know how either," she interrupted. "But I did. It happened. And it was real. I saw him. I heard his voice and saw his lips move. I even felt him, Ridley. He held my hand and touched my face. He even kissed me, right before he left. Right before you came in."

"But, how—"

"I don't know, Ridley, but you can't tell anyone. He made me promise. He'd kill me if he knew I told you. Promise me," she demanded, her expression serious.

"Alright. I promise," I agreed. Then I thought of Bo. I had to tell him, but I didn't want to out-and-out lie to Savannah. "Unless Bo comes back, too. I can tell him, right?"

Savannah grinned tolerantly. "Yes. If Bo mysteriously turns back up, you can tell him."

We were silent for a few minutes, each lost in thought.

"So, did he say where he's been? What happened?"

"No, he told me he'd find me later and we'd talk more."

"Why is he back now? I mean, where has he been?"

Savannah shrugged.

"All he said was that he could finally trust himself around me, whatever that means."

A little twinge of unease poked the back of my mind, but I was still too flabbergasted to make much sense of it right then.

"Devon's back," I said numbly. What in the world could that mean? And Savannah could actually see him. I was missing something, something important. I could feel it, but I just couldn't latch on to it.

"What are you doing in here anyway? How'd you know where to find me?"

"Dead cowboy," I answered absently.

"Dead- oh, Zach."

"Right, Zach."

"Well," Savannah said, standing abruptly. "Let's go get our freak on. We've got some rug to cut before midnight."

That shook me out of my stupor.

"I don't think there's going to be any more dancing tonight."

"Why not?"

"Bailey Adams showed up with a torn costume and blood all over her face. She's saying that Summer attacked her and Jason and then dragged Jason off."

Savannah gasped. "Shut up!"

"I'm serious."

"What- I mean, who—"

"Don't ask me. I've got nothing."

"Come on, then. Let's go see what's going on," Savannah said, grabbing my hand and tugging me forward. "Well, you can see. I'll listen."

I looked over at her and she was grinning cheekily. She was fine, right back to her old self. Nothing got Savannah down for long.

"You're impossible."

"I know," she agreed pleasantly.

The cops were just arriving as we walked back into the gym. I gave Savannah a play-by-play of what I was seeing.

"One cop's got Bailey over in the corner asking her questions. There's another one talking to Mr. Hall. The back doors are open and I can see some lights out there. I guess they're looking for Jason."

The cop that was talking to Mr. Hall strode to the center of that area marked off to be the dance floor and he stopped.

"Can I have your attention, please?" he shouted in an authoritative voice.

A hush fell over the room and every eye turned toward him.

"One of the cops is getting ready to make an announcement," I whispered to Savannah.

"I kinda figured that out," she whispered back. "I'm blind, not deaf, remember?"

"Oh," I said, feeling a sheepish grin slide into place. "Sorry."

"My name is Officer Felding and I'm going to need everyone to form a single file line in front of that table," he said, indicating the refreshments table. "I'm going to need your name, address and contact information, as well as your whereabouts for the last two hours. That includes bathroom breaks, trips to your car, any time and any reason that you were not inside this room."

He backed up toward the table, raising his arms and motioning us forward like a ground crew member at the airport, guiding a large plane into its hangar.

Kids started slowly moving forward to follow him, squeezing themselves into a thin line that snaked all the way around the gym.

The cop turned and spoke to Mr. Hall, who scrambled off quickly, obviously sent in search of something. A few minutes later, after the cop had cleared a spot on the refreshments table, Mr. Hall returned with two metal folding chairs in one hand and a stack of paper in the other.

The cop took the stack of paper and put it in on the table in front of him. He unfolded one of the chairs and sat. Mr. Hall unfolded the other and slid it under the table on the other side, opposite the policeman.

Officer Felding motioned the first student forward. It was a girl and, if the look on her face was any indication, she was scared to death. He motioned for her to sit in the chair opposite him as he began asking her questions. And so the process began. Savannah and I chatted quietly amongst ourselves and with the few others in our part of the line. Meanwhile, I scanned the shadows and the doorways, constantly watching for Bo.

I knew it would be incredibly difficult for him to contact me without being discovered. I'm sure he wished, as I did, that his invisibility was more controllable, more of an at-will condition. With fresh blood in his system, without some serious stress to burn it off, he'd be quite discernible for some time.

A shiver passed through me as I thought of him being attacked by a vampire Drew or a whatever-she-is Summer and having to fight for his life. That would increase his metabolism, but I'd rather him not gain his transparency in such a way. No one could be 100% certain yet that Bo was the boy who can't be killed, and until that could be ascertained, I didn't want him taking any chances.

Savannah was deep in conversation with one of our school band's violinists when something fluttered in my stomach. Once more, my eyes searched the periphery of the room.

I caught movement in the same hallway Bo had taken me into. Something shifted just inside the shadows. I saw the flash of a hand as it breached the light. It motioned me forward and then disappeared again. It had to be Bo. Didn't it?

I scrambled for an excuse, a good reason to escape the crowded gymnasium and make my way to Bo. I spotted another cop, standing by the double doors at the back of the gym, the ones that were propped open and now showed a string of yellow crime scene tape that passed in front of them. I concluded that they must've found something bothersome.

"I've gotta pee," I told Savannah. I waved to the policeman. "Excuse me."

His head turned toward me and he motioned me forward. I hurried toward him, smiling my most innocent, beguiling smile.

"I'm sorry, but is there any way that I could be excused for, like, five minutes to go to the bathroom?"

When he didn't immediately agree, I pressed. "Please?" I think I might even have batted my eyelashes. I can't be sure.

He looked uncomfortably at the other officer and then he sighed. I knew I had him then.

"It will only take a minute. I promise."

"Alright. Five minutes, or I'm coming in after you."

"Thank you. I'll be right back."

I hurried off, crossing the gym and bolting through the doors into the hallway. Rather than making a left, however, I veered right, toward the auditorium. I could access the small hallway from that direction, too. That must've been how Bo got in there without being seen.

I opened the auditorium door, slipped through and let it fall quietly shut behind me. The only lighting was the red glow of the three exit signs; one behind me and one over the doors on either side of the stage toward the front. I scrambled down the sloped aisle and made my way to the steps that led up onto the platform.

I turned the corner to round the curtains and go back stage. That's the only way I could get to the door that led to the gym, the door that led to Bo.

I jerked to a halt. Nothing but pitch black lay in front of me, between me and the door. A little shower of trepidation rained chills down my arms.

I listened closely for any sounds, but the only thing I heard was the muffled thump of my own heartbeat beating in my ears.

Quietly, I placed one foot in front of the other and entered the darkness. I struggled to make out shapes of things that stood in my path. Just barely, I could make out a rack that held costumes. It was pushed up against the wall. I saw the pale outline of the tall top of a cardboard castle they'd used in a set at the beginning of the school year when they'd put on Romeo and Juliet. I imagined that every high school in the free world had the exact same light gray castle turret.

I saw the thin stream of light coming from the top of the door that led to the gym and knew the short flight of stairs was straight ahead.

Then something moved in front of the light, blocking it out for an instant before it reappeared.

My heart lurched and my breath was suddenly trapped inside lungs that had ceased to work. My first thought was that something, someone—the same someone who'd attacked me in my room or the same someone who'd attacked me in the woods—was after me. What if it had been Summer all along? Or Drew?

Fear blinded my senses to everything else, so when hands grabbed my arms, I opened my mouth to scream, ready to fight like a hellcat and claw my way out of there.

A hand covered my mouth and a familiar voice had my fear draining away like storm water.

"Shh, it's me," Bo said softly. "I didn't mean to scare you."

I breathed heavily for a few seconds while all my vital signs returned to normal. "That's ok. What did you find out?"

"There was at least one vampire here, but I don't think it was a female."

"So Bailey didn't see Summer? Why would she say that?" I was immediately irritated that she might've maliciously blamed Summer for something so horrendous.

"I didn't say Summer wasn't there. I said there was at least one vampire there. But there was something else, too, something I haven't smelled before."

"Something you haven't smelled before?" I asked in surprise. I would've thought Bo would be familiar with...well, whatever else was out there. It would've bothered me more if I didn't just then remember that Bo's memory had been tampered with. A lot. "Any thoughts on what it might be?"

"Well, I keep thinking about the biting. It's not like a vampire at all. We don't chew or take out chunks of flesh."

"What does?"

"Lucius said that when vampires feed, we don't just feed on the blood; we feed on life. He said that it can have side effects, draining away someone's life like that and leaving them somewhat alive. He mentioned that it changes them, gives them a madness and a hunger of their own."

"You think that someone's been feeding on Summer?"

"I think it's possible."

"How would we know? And what would we have to do about it? I mean, is there any way to save someone like that?"

Bo shrugged helplessly. "I just don't know. I need to see Lucius."

"Then go," I encouraged. "We'll be fine."

"No. I'm staying until you get home safely. I can go later. I may even wait until you're at school on Monday."

"Bo, you don't have to—"

He put his finger to my lips. "Don't argue. I'm not leaving you."

Even though I, too, wanted answers, it warmed me, thrilled me to hear him say that.

Unbidden, the image of Bo with another girl popped into my mind, a faceless girl who was destined to be something to him that I could never be.

Angrily, I pushed the thoughts aside, determined not to let a bleak future ruin the only days I'd probably ever have with him. I refused to live anywhere but the present when it came to Bo. I'd hold onto him as long as I could and I'd relish every second.

I smiled. "Alright. What do you want me to do now, then?"

"I'll be watching. Just wait your turn and when it's time to leave, go straight to your car. Take Savannah home and I'll meet you there."

"At Savannah's? What if she—"

Bo grinned, a sexy, lopsided tilt of his lips. "Trust me, I can be very quiet when I need to be."

Flashes of our time in my bedroom and our interlude in the hall, just a few feet away, flickered through my mind and brought my blood instantly to a sizzling boil. Bo had an insane effect on me. He could block out everything else in the world, no matter how horrible or scary or important. He was like the sun in my sky, chasing away darkness and shadow. Everything melted away in the brilliance of his love.

"I shouldn't have said that," he said. I heard the telltale hissing of the Ss and I couldn't help but smile.

I stepped in close to Bo's body. I could still feel the incredible heat of him; it poured off him in scorching waves.

I reached up blindly, sliding my hand up Bo's warm chest, finding my way to his delicious lips. I traced the chiseled outline with my fingertip.

"I just wish we had time to further explore how quiet you can be."

His lips parted when he caught his breath. I slipped my finger into his mouth and rubbed gently back and forth, testing the two pointed tips of his lower teeth.

Knowing that Bo was on fire for me—for my body, for my blood—and that any minute, someone could come through that door and find us was a heady combination, dangerously seductive.

I gasped when I felt the sting of my skin breaking beneath the sharp edge of Bo's tooth. Liquid heat gushed through my body, pooling in that part of me that ached the most, the part that throbbed for Bo, for his touch.

Bo's hand shot up and his fingers wound around my wrist, pulling my finger from his mouth.

"You're playing with fire," he growled.

"I know," I whispered breathlessly.

Gently, Bo released me and set me away from him.

"You'd better go."

The air around me felt suddenly colder than ever without the heat of Bo's body so close. I felt bereft, in several ways at once. Knowing they were finite, it was harder than ever to see moments like these come to an end, especially an unsatisfying end.

A shiver passed through me, as if that feeling of loss was a precursor to the cold emptiness I'd feel when Bo moved on to an eternity with someone else.

"Ok," I said, trying not to be too obvious about my disappointment.

I turned to make my way back through the dark back stage area. I'd only walked a couple feet when I turned back to address Bo.

"Do you—"

The question died on my lips. He was already gone. I could feel it.

****

As he'd promised, I was just pulling away from the curb at Savannah's when Bo appeared at the edge of my headlight beams. He was still in his Dracula get up, the irony of which made me smile. He'd shed his mask of humanity and dressed as himself to go to a costume party.

I drove forward a few feet and stopped. With head-spinning speed, Bo was seated in the passenger side, grinning at me.

"Let's go."

I just shook my head. Nothing he did should surprise me anymore.

Several minutes later, I pulled in my driveway and cut the engine.

"You're coming in, aren't you?"

Bo looked at me skeptically.

"I don't mean, like, where my parents can see you. I just meant you're not leaving right now, are you?"

"Not if you want me to stay."

"I want you to stay," I assured him. "Give me a few minutes to get to my room and open the window, ok?"

"I'll be waiting."

The brightness from the dusk-to-dawn light at the corner of the house shone into the car, illuminating one side of Bo's handsome face. It highlighted the sharp angles and threw the other half into deep shadow. With my fingers on the door handle, I paused, taking in his beauty, his masculine perfection. I wanted to memorize the way he looked at that exact moment, to let the image sear itself on my brain so that I'd never forget how gorgeous he was and that, for a while, he was all mine.

When his brow wrinkled in confusion, I gave him a shaky smile and slipped quietly out of the car. I didn't need him to start asking questions.

I opened the front door as quietly as I could, hoping to get past Mom and Dad unnoticed, just in case they weren't asleep. Only that didn't happen.

"Ridley, is that you?"

Dad.

"Yeah, Dad. I'm home," I said, veering toward the living room to poke my head in.

"How'd it go?"

"Just fine," I said, leaving out…everything.

"You sure about that?" Dad asked, getting up off the couch and walking over to stand in front of me. He stopped and crossed his arms over his chest, a very intimidating stance.

"Yeah, why?"

"One of your teachers called here tonight to make sure that you got home alright."

"What? Why?"

"Apparently there was some commotion at the dance, a couple of kids got attacked. Is that right?"

I sighed, rolling my eyes. "Yes, but it's not what you think."

"Then why did you tell me everything was fine, young lady?"

"Because I didn't want to worry you over something like that until the police had a chance to figure out what happened."

"The police were there?"

"Well, yeah. Mr. Hall called them and, when they came, they wanted to get some information from all the students."

"What happened? Exactly."

"A girl, Bailey Adams, showed up saying that another girl at our school attacked her boyfriend and dragged him off. They're thinking that either she made it up or someone played a prank on her. It wasn't a big deal, Dad."

"Anything that involves the police is a big deal. And for one of your teachers to call here to check on you, that's an even bigger deal. Obviously she thought you might be in danger." Dad rubbed his hand over the back of his neck. "I swear, Ridley, what am I going to do with you? You have to be more careful."

"I was, Dad. We weren't in any danger or they wouldn't have let us leave."

"Then why did Ms. Bowman call here?"

"Ms. Bowman?"

"Yes, your, um, I forgot what subject she said she taught."

"Are you sure her name was Bowman?"

I didn't have a teacher by that name. In fact, I couldn't think of any teacher at the school with the last name of Bowman.

"Yes, Ridley. Heather Bowman."

I felt the blood drain from my face. Heather Bowman? I knew of only one Heather, and that was the Heather. And the only Bowman that I knew was Bo.

"Oh, yeah, Ms. Bowman," I said as casually as I could muster. "What exactly did she say?"

"Just that she was calling to check on you. She wanted to make sure you were at home, out of harm's way."

Was that some sort of message? Or had she been trying to find out where I was?

"Ok, well, I'm tired. I'm going to bed," I announced, throwing in a fake yawn for good measure. I was so wired at that very moment that the only thing that would've induced sleep was either a horse tranquilizer or a Taser.

"Ridley, please be more careful," Dad pleaded, his voice dropping low so that only I could hear him. "I don't think your mother could survive it if something happened to you, too."

I had to agree with him. She probably couldn't. Of course, she was doing a pretty good job of numbing herself up against life, so it was possible that we were both dead wrong.

"I know, Dad. I promise to be more careful."

That was the best tack to take with them: submissive agreement. Don't rock the boat, especially a boat as unstable as ours.

I held Dad's gaze, my most genuine expression in place, until I saw that I'd convinced him of my sincerity.

His lips twitched in a tiny grin. "Good," he said, brushing his hand over my hair. "You look beautiful. Did I tell you that?"

"No, but thanks."

"Come here," he said, pulling me to him for a hug. "I love you, Ridley."

I was stunned by both his display of affection as well as his admission. Our family didn't act like this anymore, hadn't since Izzy died. I felt stiff in his arms. It had been so long since either of them had shown me affection this way, especially sober, that I wasn't quite sure how to be comfortable with it now. I wanted to melt into his arms, to enjoy the comfort that I'd missed for so long, but I just couldn't. It felt strange and forced and bitter. I ended up patting his back mechanically, wishing for the moment to be over.

"I love you, too, Dad."

When he let me go, I tried to smile as I turned to walk to my bedroom, but I felt like it was glaringly obvious that I was off kilter.

Once in my room, I rushed to the window and threw it open and raised the screen. I stuck my head out and heard a rustling in the bush to the left. Bo stepped out from behind it and I backed up so he could climb through. He did it with such speed and ease, it looked as if he was outside one minute and inside the next. No transition, no movement, no distance between point A and point B.

I thought of my attacker and how I didn't stand a chance against someone like that—a vampire— who wanted to hurt me. There would be no keeping her out, no escaping her if she got in. If a vampire wanted to hurt me, there was little I could do to prevent it.

"I need to change. Do you mind?" I asked as I walked to my dresser to get out some pajamas.

Bo stepped over to stand behind me, in front of the mirror that sat on top of the shiny mahogany surface. I watched his reflection as he raised his hand and pushed my hair back from one side of my neck and bent his head to place a kiss right at the curve of my shoulder.

"I don't mind," he said beside my ear. "In fact, I could be convinced to lend a hand if you need help getting out of this dress."

One hand brushed down my back and his fingers settled at the top of my zipper. Though goose bumps erupted all over my chest and shoulders, my mind was running over a thousand worrisome things, not the least of which was that it was high time Bo and I talked. Even his intoxicating presence, his alluring scent, his arousing heat couldn't compete with the heaviness of my heart.

"I think I can handle this one on my own," I said, watching his reaction in the mirror.

Bo raised his head and his eyes met mine in the mirror. I stared at him, and he stared back. For a moment, all I could think about was how he was so perfect it hurt. But in that brief wordless exchange, Bo came to understand that something was wrong. I saw the weight settle over him like an invisible iron blanket. I recognized it, knew it well; it was dread.

He nodded and stepped back to let me move on to the bathroom, where I quickly changed into my pajamas and then went back out to my closet to hang up my dress.

Bo was lounging on the bed, but he looked anything but relaxed. There was a tightness about him, a readiness that reminded me of a coiled spring.

I sat on the bed in front of Bo, facing him, and curled my feet up under me.

"I got a call tonight."

"I heard. Ms. Bowman, right?"

I nodded.

"So ,what's the problem?"

"I don't have a teacher by the name of Bowman."

Bo shrugged. "Maybe it was just a teacher, not your teacher, calling to check on the kids from the dance."

"Bo, there isn't a teacher in the entire school with the last name of Bowman. And did you hear her first name?"

"Hea—" he began, but then stopped suddenly, sitting up. "The Heather?"

"I don't know, but I would imagine so."

Bo leapt off the bed, a movement so fast it didn't even shake the bed. He began to pace my bedroom floor like a caged animal.

"These past weeks, I haven't been able to find out anything about her. Why would she call you? What did she say?"

"Just that she was calling to check on me, see if I was at home. She wanted to make sure I was 'out of harm's way'."

"That means she's close."

"Why would you say that?"

"Just trust me. She's close. Now if I could just find her…"

"Bo, there's something else that you need to know about Heather."

He stopped his pacing, looking at me expectantly, his eyes full of that anxiety that says I don't want to know, but I have to find out.

"While it's true that she was probably the one who had something to do with orchestrating your father's death, I think...we think...that it might be much bigger than that."

"We?"

"Me and Lucius."

Bo's eyes narrowed on me. "What is it that you think is going on?"

"Bo, Lucius has kept some things from you because he wasn't quite sure what to make of...you. I'm sure you've wondered how you survived the poisoning."

Bo nodded. "I figured the stories were wrong. I thought since it had never been done before, that it was just assumed that it would be deadly, that no one really knew for sure. Why? What do you know about that?"

"There's a legend, one I don't really know that much about, but it tells of a boy who can't be killed."

Easily reaching the obvious conclusion, Bo said, "And you think that person is me?"

"Well, it certainly looks like it could be."

"Just because the poison didn't kill me? That's hardly enough—"

"That's not all."

"Alright," he said slowly, uneasily. "What else?"

"This boy, he's special. It's only him that can't be killed because his destiny in life is to kill his father, the first of the vampires."

"Well, I know my father wasn't a vampire, so I don't see how this could have anything to do with me."

"Unless that wasn't your real father."

Bo's gaze sharpened, his nostrils flaring in agitation.

"Of course he was my father."

"Bo, do you remember telling me that Lucius found you, that you'd made your way to his cabin after the vampires attacked you and your father?"

"Yeah. Why?"

I picked at my fingernails nervously. "When Lucius found you, you weren't human."

"I know. I'd been bitten."

"Lucius says that you weren't newly turned either."

"What? But that's not possible. I remember exactly what happened."

I got up and walked to Bo, feeling the need to comfort him as I told him things that would tear apart the only world he'd ever known. Or at least the only one he could remember.

"But are you sure that they actually happened?"

"Of course I'm sure. I saw them."

"Bo, what if someone had fed you blood? What if someone was controlling your mind?"

"But that's impossible. There's no—"

"Are you sure?"

"It would take someone incredibly powerful to pull off something like that, someone—"

"As powerful as, say, the very first vampire?"

"Ridley, that's ridiculous. Even if it were possible, I have a life. You can't fabricate an entire life."

"What? You mean give you memories of a childhood or playing football? Memories of fishing with your dad?"

Bo stepped back from me angrily. "My life was more than that. I have a mother, too, remember?"

I closed my eyes against the pain that I could already see in his. Something deep inside him knew that what I was saying could be true, could be.

"Bo, she doesn't remember you."

I kept my eyes shut, but I had no trouble imagining the hurt that was in Bo's dark, fathomless eyes. An invisible fist squeezed my heart. I never wanted to hurt Bo, but he needed to know this in case it was true. Because, if it was, his life was in danger in ways that we never could've imagined, ways more powerful and treacherous than anything we ever could've thought.

"What?" His voice was quiet, wounded. I didn't need to see his face to know that he was in agony.

"Bo, I'm so sorry," I said, my voice breaking on the last.

I turned my face away, eyes still closed. I couldn't bear to look at him, could hardly stand to be in the same room with him, his pain was so palpable. My arms ached to hold him, so I wrapped them around myself. He didn't want my comfort right now, no matter how much I wanted to give it.

I said nothing, determined to let him absorb what I'd said in his own time. When the silence stretched on and on and on, I finally opened my eyes.

I was alone.

CHAPTER SEVEN

Why police think the killings have stopped in Southmoore. Sunday's top story coming up next...

"Turn that up, Ridley," Dad said over a bite of his cinnamon roll.

I slid out of my chair and grabbed the remote off the counter and hit the volume button a few times. I set it down beside my plate and continued munching on my own breakfast. I had been trying to ignore the news. Not only did I not want to hear any more bad news; I really didn't think it was good for digestion.

The one good thing the day had going for it, bad news included, was the distraction a Sunday would provide, at least for a little while. And a little was better than none. I'd take it. I'd take anything that would help me get my mind off of Bo and the distress I knew he was in.

Every time I thought about him, about the devastation he must be feeling, I got queasy. It didn't take me long last night to discover that I'd rather be beaten or shot than to hurt Bo. I honestly believe that it was more painful for me to hurt Bo, to see him hurting, than it was for me to be hurt. I know that sounds ridiculous; in a way it felt ridiculous, too, but the more time that passed, the more I realized that it was true. His anguish was killing me on the inside, eating away at me, gnawing constantly at my guts.

I still had the same bite of pastry in my mouth when the commercials ended and the news reporter's voice grabbed all of our attention. It brought me back to the present, reminding me to chew and swallow. I figure that anchorman might've saved me from choking to death on my food.

Southmoore Police Chief Edwin McDonnahough released a statement early yesterday morning citing the area's most recent crime statistics. Most impressive was the decrease in murders, violent attacks and missing persons reports. McDonnahough credits the reduction in violence to the supposed disappearance of the Southmoore Slayer. He believes the improved numbers are a direct result of the collaborative efforts of the Slayer Task Force.

While neighboring towns are openly supportive of the Task Force's progress, many deny that they will rest easy until the Slayer is captured. That certainly seems to be the case here in Harker.

Despite the presence of the Task Force in the Harker Community, violence is up almost sixty-five percent compared to last year, with an one hundred-twenty percent increase in missing persons reports. Harker Police Department spokesperson Gloria Ashton released a statement assuring citizens that law enforcement officials are doing everything they can to increase safety measures around the community. Some speculate that the Southmoore Slayer has moved south, continuing his violent reign of terror here in Harker. Police deny that recent attacks are the work of the Slayer, citing the FBI's psychological profile of the killer's modus operandi, which behaviorists believe does not change during the course of a spree.

The parents of the most recent people to disappear are not convinced, however, as they wait by the phone day after day, hoping for news of the return of their loved ones.

In addition to the disappearance of four local high school children earlier this year, four more have gone missing since Friday, an alarming number when compared to the rate of abduction in Southmoore during the Slayer's reign. Local teens Drew Connors, Aisha Williams, and Summer Collins were last seen Friday night, though Summer Collins has been officially listed as a Person of Interest in the recent abduction of Jason Gwynn. Police are currently withholding any additional information about Gwynn's disappearance, as it is part of an ongoing violent attack investigation. If you see any of these children, please call the number at the bottom of the screen immediately…

Giving up on my breakfast, I tossed my roll back onto my plate, pushed my chair back and took my dishes to the sink.

"I'm going to get in the shower," I said as I made my way from the kitchen.

All I got in response was a grunt and a nod. My parents' eyes were glued to the television, watching the faces of the missing flash by. After they'd shown photographs of the most recently disappeared, they showed school pictures of Trinity and Devon, and then showed some vague snapshots of Bo and Lars. Neither of them had been around long enough for an official school photo. I'm sure it was probably an accident that anyone had a picture of them at all. With cell phone cameras now, though, it would be nearly impossible to regulate the capture of images.

Not that it mattered. The pictures barely even looked like Bo and Lars. They were blurry and distant, which was probably a good thing. If Lucius was right, it would be terrible for another of Bo's many lives to come back to haunt him. It's hard to tell how many towns across the country could have him listed as a missing person.

Later, at church, I found that I was becoming increasingly distracted, my mind flitting between missing friends, a crumbling life and the pain of ten thousand questions that surrounded the person that I loved most on the planet.

The sermon was about submitting to the will of God, a subject that was particularly distasteful to me at the moment. Giving up your wants in favor of someone else's, even if that someone was divine and all-powerful, wasn't easy. In fact, it went totally against the grain. On top of that, the thought that God would let me love Bo so much, all the while knowing that He'd hand-crafted another girl specifically for him, made me crazy. More than once, I found myself praying that He'd let me be that girl, that somehow, some way, He would cosmically rearrange things so that I could be the one for Bo.

I felt like a basket case by the time we pulled back into the driveway. After changing out of my church clothes and into jeans and a hooded sweatshirt, there was still no sign of Bo, no word. So I decided that, rather than sit in my room and fester, I would go see Lucius.

As I walked out, Mom and Dad were talking quietly in the living room. The television wasn't on; they were simply sitting on the couch facing one another as if they were making important decisions. I should've known that didn't bode well for me.

"I'm going out for a while," I said, moving off quickly in hopes of escaping without another word.

"Wait a minute, Ridley. We need to talk to you."

We?

Rolling my eyes toward the ceiling, I resisted the urge to say aloud, What now? Instead, I turned back toward the living room and leaned against the doorjamb, adopting my most innocently interested expression.

"What's up?"

"Your mother and I have been discussing this and, I know you're not going to like it, but for a while, we don't want you going anywhere by yourself after dark."

Their timing couldn't have been worse to start being caring and parental.

"What? But Dad—"

"Ridley," he interrupted, holding up his hand. "This is not open for discussion. It is getting too dangerous for you to be out there alone after dark. I'm sorry, but this is the way it's going to be."

"Well, how long is 'a while'?"

"Until they either catch whoever's behind this or things settle down."

"But that could be months."

"Well, I'm sorry, Ridley, but you're just going to have to make adjustments. You surely can't expect us to just let you go gallivanting around when your friends are disappearing, can you?"

"Dad, I'm careful. I don't take stupid chances like they do."

Even as I spoke the words, I felt the condemnation of having told them an out-and-out lie. I took insane chances all the time by doing things like going into the woods, woods known to be dangerous, by myself to see a vampire.

I doubted anyone could argue that there were few activities that were riskier.

Dad shook his head. "I know you're a good kid, Ridley, and a smart one. That's not the point. We're simply not willing to take the chance that you could be next. Period."

I started to argue, but Dad had that not-another-word expression that told me I was starting to tread on thin ice. The last thing I needed was to get myself grounded. I silently reminded myself that Dad would be gone tomorrow and Mom would be back off the wagon, so the restriction was temporary—more temporary than they knew.

"Fine," I huffed. "So what, I can't be out after dark unless I'm with friends? Is that it?"

"Well, let's just start with being home before dark and we'll take it on a case-by-case basis."

"Dad." I stopped myself, biting my tongue and clamping my lips shut in a tight line. "Fine. I'll be back before dark then."

I spun on my heel and hurried away before they could start asking questions or give me any more ridiculous limitations. I'd have to make today count, inasmuch as making the most of my time with Lucius and trying to find Bo.

By the time I'd made my way through the woods and was mounting the steps to Lucius's cabin, I was spitting-mad. It seemed as though life was just bound and determined to work against me at every turn. I was in desperate need of a pity party and today felt like a good day to throw it.

Fortunately, Lucius was home. And fully clothed. Unfortunately, Bo wasn't there, though he had been. I'd apparently just missed him. He'd spent the majority of the night with Lucius and then run off to "think." I tried to quell the sense of dread that caused me. Bo running off to "think" didn't bode well. That had a tendency to end up with Bo wanting to leave in order to save the rest of us from…everything.

"What did Bo want to talk about?" I asked Lucius as he poked at the flaming logs burning in the huge fireplace in his below-ground quarters.

"As you can imagine, lass, he was very upset about his parents. I'm sure you would be, too if someone told you that everything you thought you knew, everything you thought was real was all just a lie. He's lost all the people that he loved, all the family he's ever known."

"Well, hopefully not everyone he loved," I said quietly, miserably.

"I was referring to his parents, his entire life."

"I know, I just…"

"What? What is it, lovely Ridley? You look concerned."

"I just can't get that story out of my mind."

"What story?"

"The one about the girl that's fated to be with the boy who can't be killed."

"Lass, there's so much we don't know, don't bother yourself with things like that now. There are many more important matters to be thinking about."

"Such as?"

Lucius replaced the poker into its stand beside the hearth and turned to take a seat in an armchair to my right.

"Such as who's attacking you and why, what's going on with all these children, and how to control the other creatures."

"Other creatures? What other creatures?"

"You remember me telling you what can happen when a vampire drinks from a human, don't you?"

"Yeah, they become sort of like zombies or something, right?"

"Well, that's quite a theatrical exaggeration, but I think you get the gist of it, yes."

"What about them?"

"We've got to find and kill them, lass, before they become a real problem."

"Kill them? You have to kill them?"

"There's no other choice. Once so much life is gone from them, they cease to be the person that they were. I thought I explained that they become vicious and mindless, hungry beyond control."

"You did, but I didn't realize that- that—"

I didn't realize that there was no hope for them, that death was the only recourse.

I thought of how many times Bo had fed from me, and I wondered how long I had until I became...something else.

"So then what do we do?"

"Well, we first have to find them. For a while, they can blend into the general population fairly well. It's as the madness progresses that they become easier to spot."

"And what do you have to do when you find them? I mean, how do you," I paused to swallow, nearly choking on the words. "Kill them?"

"It's not as easy as one might think. The loss of life makes them harder, physically and emotionally. Their conscience recedes as their tissues degenerate. Physically, they become hardened, almost petrified, like a fossil. Makes them very difficult to destroy."

He didn't really answer my question. "How do you kill them then?" I asked, hating to repeat myself.

"They must be decapitated and their heads obliterated."

That was what he was trying to keep from me: the awful reality of how brutally their lives must end.

"So, what, use an ax or a knife to cut- cut—"

My stomach sloshed with the thought of taking someone's head off using a knife, of sawing through their skin and sinew as they bled and struggled. Saliva rushed to my mouth.

"That would never work. Only older, more powerful vampires can do it, as their heads must be torn off. No blade would work, no weapon."

Bile gurgled in my throat. Torn off? And I thought the knife thing was bad!

"Alright, can we please change the subject?"

"You asked. I was merely obliging—"

"I know I asked, but I- I didn't know…"

We sat in silence for a few minutes while I struggled to rid my mind of the gruesome images of decapitation that I couldn't seem to stop picturing.

When finally I spoke, I decided to go with a subject change.

"Lucius, are the legends and stories of vampires and the boy who can't be killed recorded anywhere? Or are they just sort of handed down, generation to generation, like ghost stories?"

Lucius cocked his head to one side in thought.

"If I'm not mistaken, there is a book that supposedly details many of the myths surrounding the origin of the vampire. However, I wouldn't know where to even begin a search for such a book."

"Do you remember what it was called?"

He rubbed his chin as he thought.

"No. It is said to be written in an old language, one few alive would know how to read. If one is to believe in such a book, though, then one must believe in the letter of Iofiel as well."

"What's that?"

"Supposedly, after Iofiel was captured and returned to God, she overheard God's plan to take her lover's life and she wrote a letter to him, detailing the only way that he might take his son's life, thereby sparing his own. Legend says that it took Iofiel hundreds of years to find out where her love was and get the letter delivered to him."

"You're saying that there is a way that Bo can be killed? I mean, assuming that Bo is the boy who can't be killed."

"So the story says."

"Doesn't that sort of —"

"I know it makes no sense, but I would imagine that, as with most things in life, where there's a will there's a way. Some sort of loophole maybe."

"And where is this letter now?"

"I would assume that the fallen angel is in possession of it."

"Has anyone ever found out what it says?"

"Not that I've ever heard. It's my understanding that the letter wasn't delivered so very long ago, only a few decades."

"If that's the case, then why haven't they killed Bo?"

Lucius shrugged. "Your guess is as good as mine."

I stood and walked to the fireplace, looking into the yellow-orange flames for answers, but finding none. I was more frustrated than I could ever remember being.

The book that was at Sebastian's house could very well be the book that Lucius was referring to. But without the letter from Iofiel, it was no help to me whatsoever. It only told me their history, not what information I needed to secure our future. Of course, if I was the girl destined to help Bo, I might know a little something more about that, something divinely inspired.

"If Bo is that boy, will he ever be able to remember the things that he's supposed to know about killing his father?"

"It's hard to say. If his father has been feeding him blood to control his mind, alter his remembrance, all this time, it may have permanently affected his memory."

"Then how—"

"The girl," Lucius said simply.

I turned to look at him. His face was blank, an inscrutable mask. For a moment, I hated him for bringing her up, but, then again, I'd asked.

"So, in a way, she's the key to it all."

Lucius nodded curtly.

I was angry—inordinately and irrationally angry—giving me the sudden urge to put Lucius and his disturbing tales behind me, at least for the time being. There was no escaping them forever if I thought to help Bo and keep him in my life for a little while longer, but there was nothing I could do today. So I was walking away.

"Thanks for your help," I said sharply, turning a tight smile on Lucius and heading for the door.

"I know it's not what you want to hear," Lucius began, but I cut him off.

"No, but I guess it's what I need to hear, right?" I laughed bitterly and opened the door. "See you, Lucius."

I stomped the entire way back to my car, giving myself a bone deep ache in my lower back by the time I was sitting behind the wheel.

"Smart, Ridley. Very smart," I chastised in the silence of my car.

I pulled off the side of the shoulder and onto the road, blasting the radio, determined to drown out all the nasty voices in my head, all the hopelessness and despair that was threatening to overtake me.

The first station I turned to was playing a country song about needing someone in the middle of the night. When the first five or six bars made me want to cry, I switched the channel.

The next song I stopped on was singing about not being strong enough to stand in someone's arms without falling at their feet.

Click, click, click. I quickly turned the dial. That one made me want to drive my car right off the road.

Every single station I landed on was playing something sad or depressing. I decided to abandon the radio in favor of a CD, but I'd forgotten that the last band I'd chosen was one that reminded me of Bo. I ended up turning the music off completely, deciding I'd be better off listening to the silence than music that made me feel all the more. I didn't want to feel at all. I wanted mind-numbing, heart-blocking distraction.

By the time I arrived back at my house, my mood was sourer than ever. I had every intention of just going straight back to my room, but Mom called out to me before I could get the door closed.

"There's a message in here for you."

I wanted to respond with I don't care, but that would only further aggravate matters, so I turned from my door and walked back to the living room.

"From who?"

"Sebastian Aiello."

"Oh." At least it could've been a good message. "What did he want?"

"He didn't have your cell number, so he called here. He said that you two had talked about something for tonight."

I had all but forgotten. I wanted to growl.

"Yeah, he mentioned something about it, but he was supposed to call me."

"I just told you he did."

I gritted my teeth.

"I meant sooner than now. Like yesterday."

"Well, as I said, you didn't give him your cell number so..."

I sighed. "What time?"

"From eight until about eleven, he said."

I was feeling prickly and saw an opportunity to be difficult, so I took it.

"Well, I guess you'll have to call him and tell him that I can't, since I can't be out after dark." I couldn't hide my satisfied smirk.

"I told him we'd been concerned about all the violence. He's going to pick you up at 7:30 and he'll bring you home when he gets back."

Her smile was slight, but the gleam in her eye was nothing short of victorious. I wanted to scream. I just couldn't win!

"Great," I said, too brightly. I'd be darned if I let her see that she'd ruffled my feathers. I refused to give her the perverse satisfaction. "I could use some extra money. I'll be ready."

With that, I turned to walk calmly back to my room. Somehow, I even managed to resist slamming the door. Maybe I had more self-control that I thought.

It only took about half an hour of trying to occupy myself with music and magazines to realize that it was going to take something much more involved to distract me. That's when I decided to clean out my closet. And then my drawers. And then rearrange my furniture.

I worked like the devil was after me until Mom knocked on my door at 7:26, informing me that Sebastian had arrived.

We both looked down at my soiled clothes and she said disapprovingly, "I'll tell him you'll be out in just a few minutes."

I was almost relieved for it to be time to do something else. I welcomed the consuming diversion of Lilly, so I quickly changed clothes and ran the brush through my hair and headed out to meet Sebastian.

I nearly tripped over my feet when I saw him standing in the foyer. He was simply beautiful. It's not that I was attracted to him per se; I had eyes for only one guy and that guy was Bo. It was more that he was just…breathtaking. Almost painfully perfect. I'm pretty sure that a specimen like Sebastian was used by Michelangelo when he carved David.

Tonight, he was wearing a tuxedo and he looked marvelous. His gleaming skin shone against the stark white collar of his shirt and his shoulders looked impossibly wide. His blond hair was combed neatly away from his forehead, but had fallen rakishly, rebelliously to one side.

When he saw me, he smiled and I felt a flush heat my cheeks.

"Ready?"

I nodded.

"I really appreciate you helping me out like this," he said, opening the door for me.

"No problem," I said, brushing past him to step outside.

"Becky," he said, turning back to address my mother, who hadn't moved an inch and still hadn't closed her mouth all the way. "Thanks for letting me borrow her."

Mom smiled, a dazed sort of smile that made me want to laugh. I'd say Sebastian had that effect on a lot of women.

Probably some men, too. Children, animals, plants—I doubted there were many organisms immune to his charm and charisma.

Purring quietly in the driveway was a glossy black sedan that looked ridiculously expensive. I didn't know much about cars, but only an idiot wouldn't have known that this one cost a pretty penny. Several, in fact.

He opened my door for me and closed it behind me once I was seated. It closed with a muffled thump that whispered money into the silent interior. The sound of my car door closing was vaguely reminiscent of a nickel hitting the bottom of a tuna can—cheap and tinny.

I inhaled. The car still had that new smell that I loved. I'd tried the air freshener called "new car scent" before, but it smelled more like an old plastic trash bag than this: the real deal.

Sebastian opened the door and folded his long legs behind the steering wheel, shifted into gear and then we were off.

He chatted politely on the short trip, sticking to small-talk topics like school and weather. When we arrived, Lilly was waiting for me, so I barely spoke to him as he left. He merely reminded me that he'd made fresh lemonade, his number was on the fridge and that he'd be back by eleven.

Lilly was dressed in a pink princess nightgown and itty bitty high heel slippers. A tiara was on her crown, nestled in her thick auburn hair. She was gorgeous.

With great pomp and circumstance, she ushered me into her playroom where she had arranged an elaborate tea with several of her favorite stuffed animals, including Pia the polar bear and Lenny the llama.

She showed me my seat and I perched carefully on the edge of the little wooden chair, careful not to put too much of my weight on it.

In an oh-so-adult way, Lilly proceeded to make introductions.

"Nice to meet you, Mrs. Bear and Mr. Llama," I said, reaching out to shake their furry feet.

"They're married, so they both have the same last name," Lilly informed me.

Lilly's perfectly articulated words and quick mind were amazing to me. It had been a long time since I'd been around children, but I was pretty sure she was extremely advanced to be just shy of four.

"Oh, I'm sorry. Mr. and Mrs. Llama, then."

She nodded, satisfied with my correction.

"This is Mr. Mallard," she said, indicating the duck that sat to her right. "And this is his daughter, Lilly," she explained, pointing to the duckling that was squished into a tiny high chair across the pink plastic table from me.

"It's nice to meet you, Lilly. I love your name," I said, winking at the real Lilly. She smiled prettily.

"She's happy to meet you, but she misses her mother."

There was a hint of sadness in Lilly's silvery blue eyes and I felt the pinch of a frown between my eyes. I purposely smoothed it.

The characters at tonight's tea party were much different than the ones from the other night. I couldn't help but wonder why these had so much more emotional depth, what Lilly was thinking of and why.

I had no idea why Lilly's mother wasn't in the picture. No one had ever mentioned her, but now, considering tonight's cast of characters, I was more than a little curious.

"She does? What happened to her mother?"

I watched Lilly fiddle with the big red bow around the duckling's neck, a very maternal gesture. I wanted to ask a thousand questions, but I couldn't let myself forget that she was just a child, just a baby really.

Then something occurred to me: I'd heard of therapists using stuffed animals in children's sessions before. I couldn't see why I shouldn't give it a try.

"What happened to your mother, Lilly?" I asked, careful to address my question to the duck Lilly, not the real Lilly.

Lilly just shrugged, putting a white handkerchief in the duckling's lap like a napkin. When she began to pour tea, evidently having no intention of answering my question, I took a different tack.

"What about you, Mr. Mallard? What happened to Lilly's mother?"

"Her daddy doesn't talk about it. But he's sad. He loved his Mrs. Mallard and wishes he could see her every day."

Lilly was twisting my heart around her teeny tiny finger and she didn't even know it. I wanted to gather her in my arms and make her pain go away.

"One day, maybe Mr. Mallard will find someone else he loves just as much and Lilly will love her, too, and she can be a part of their family," I offered tenderly.

Oh, how I hoped that could happen for sweet Lilly!

Lilly's perfect cupid's-bow mouth rounded into a silent "oh", her shimmering eyes widening in excitement as she looked toward me.

"Could you marry Mr. Mallard? You could be Lilly's new momma."

If possible, my heart squeezed even tighter.

"I'm not a duck. I couldn't marry Mr. Mallard."

"But Lilly likes you."

"And I like Lilly. It's just that Mr. Mallard needs another duck. So does Lilly. And one day, Mr. Mallard will find that perfect duck and they'll get married and then Lilly and her family can live happily ever after."

Lilly sighed, chewing at her lip. "I guess," she said, nodding in agreement. But I wasn't convinced. Her expression said that she didn't have any hope that her family would ever be whole again.

How could a child so young, so sweet, have so much adult despair in her big beautiful eyes? What had happened in her short life to put it there? What tragedy had stolen the bliss of her youth?

With a resilience that only the innocent can manage, Lilly snapped right out of her melancholy and began presiding over her tea party as only a princess can. I laughed more than once at her charming performance and quick mind. I was rapidly discovering that she was a truly amazing child.

Lilly took a break from hosting to watch some cartoons. I sat on the couch opposite her, but it wasn't long until she climbed down from hers and walked over to mine, crawling up to sit beside me.

As we watched the animated adventures of Dora, Lilly inched her way closer and closer to me until her head was in my lap and her thumb was nestled squarely in her mouth.

I reached down to brush a few chestnut strands away from her cheek and her soft, sweet baby scent wafted up to my nose. Her lids began to blink more slowly until they dropped and didn't rise again.

Her tiny shoulders rose and fell with her deep, even breathing and I thought I could actually feel her wiggling her way into my heart and making herself a place there.

I waited a few minutes, letting her get good and asleep before moving her, then I picked her up and carried her to her bed, tucking her snugly beneath her Princess Jasmine comforter.

After I'd put her to bed, I wandered aimlessly through the house. At the front of my mind were two things: that book in Sebastian's office and the way I lost time the last time I was here.

It made me uneasy to think about, especially since I still wasn't sure what had happened. I was grateful that it hadn't happened since then, and I hoped that it wouldn't again. But in some strange way, because I hadn't blacked out like that again, I seemed to be blaming the book for that first occurrence. For that reason, irrational though it was, I was hesitant to go to the book again.

I was flipping idly through a magazine when Sebastian returned home. He looked exactly as dapper as he had when he'd left, not the least bit wrinkled or mussed.

He walked straight into the den, removing his cuff links as he walked. He flopped down on the couch Lilly had first occupied and leaned his head back against the cushions.

He exhaled in an exhausted puff and said tiredly, "I hate formal events."

I had no idea what to say to that, not having been to anything more important than prom last year. I did, however, feel really guilty that he had to take me home now.

"You know, since you're tired, I can call my parents for a ride."

Sebastian raised his head, frowning. "Absolutely not. It's no trouble and I'm not that tired."

I nodded, still feeling terrible about it.

"How did Lilly do?"

I smiled. "Great. She's an amazing little girl."

I thought of the odd beginning to our tea party, but said nothing. It was not my place and none of my business. That was one curiosity I'd have to take extra pains in squelching.

"She is something else," he declared proudly. "So, no more questions about the book?"

I was confused for all of about thirty seconds and then my mouth dropped open.

"P-pardon?"

"Last time, you paused the movie to bombard me with questions as soon as I came in the door. And tonight? Nothing," he said, grinning.

My mind was awhirl. I'd asked Sebastian questions about the book? Now, as bothersome as it was that I'd blacked out, I'd found something even more frustrating about the whole thing: I had asked questions about the book and, I would assume, had gotten some answers. Now, how was I ever going to know what I'd learned?

I put my magazine to the side and sat up straighter. "You didn't mind?"

"Are you kidding? Mythology isn't just my profession, it's my passion. It's nice to see that someone else has an interest. Ask away," he offered.

Of course, I wanted so badly to ask him a thousand questions, but if I asked the same ones I'd already asked, he'd think I was insane. More than he probably already did, that is.

"Actually, I probably need to do some research before I ask any more questions. You know, so that I know what I'm talking about." I smiled sheepishly, hoping he wouldn't suspect anything out of the way.

"Sure, sure. Anytime you want to talk..."

"Thanks. I appreciate that."

We fell into a bit of an uncomfortable silence, which Sebastian broke when he slapped his knees and stood.

"Well, I guess you'd like to go home sometime tonight, huh?"

"Whenever you're ready," I replied amicably, standing also.

When Sebastian turned toward the kitchen, making his way to the door that led to the garage, I spoke up, concerned. "Um," I began uncertainly. "What about Lilly?"

Was he just going to leave her alone in the house, unattended, with no idea where he'd gone if she awakened?

"Our housekeeper's here," he said nonchalantly.

"Oh, I didn't know you had a housekeeper."

Not only had I not seen her, Lilly hadn't mentioned her either.

"She stays in her room mostly when she's not busy."

"Oh," I responded, not knowing what else to say. It felt a little weird, knowing that someone had been lurking about the entire time I'd been in the house without me knowing it. It gave me the creeps for some reason, especially since there was a large portion of my last visit that I couldn't remember.

I followed Sebastian to the car and he drove me home. We were both silent the whole way.

When he pulled up to the curb in front of my house, he reached into his pocket and pulled out his money clip, peeling another hundred dollar bill off the top.

"I really appreciate you taking care of Lilly for me," he said sincerely, handing me the money.

"That's too much," I said, pushing his hand away. "You weren't gone that long."

"Here, take it," he said, grabbing my fingers and winding them around the bill. His hand was warm and strong, but soft. Almost too soft. "I want you to have it."

I didn't want to argue too much about it, so I thanked him and got out of the car. He didn't drive off right away. He waited until I was inside before leaving.

Mom and Dad had waited up for me.

"How'd it go?" Mom asked.

"Just fine," I said, drawing my arms up in an exaggerated stretch. "I think I'm going to go on to bed. I'm pretty tired."

They both nodded. I didn't think I'd get much argument from them.

Once in my room, I brushed my teeth and washed my face, changed into my pajamas, the whole nighttime ritual. As I was shutting the bathroom light off, I gazed around my empty bedroom, feeling lonely and melancholy. I didn't often miss my old life, but there were times when I longed for the simple problems that I used to have, the ones that I thought were earth-shattering. Oh, how perspective changes!

I lay down in my bed, resisting the urge to soothe myself with the tricks I used to use, like turning on the television or opening the window. It was starting to feel like a way of hiding from reality, from my problems, and that wouldn't do me any good. Maybe I needed to cowboy up and face them, think about them, figure out a way to solve them. I couldn't very well do that if I completely avoided them.

When I'd pulled the covers up to my chin and found myself staring blankly at the ceiling, I felt the draw of the familiar, of the one thing, the one person that consumed me.

I turned my head on the pillow to look at the window. There was no one outside it, but I knew Bo was close. I could still feel him that certainly. I pushed the covers back and walked over to the window. With my hands resting lightly on the sill, I looked out into the dark night. And I waited.

In less than a minute, I saw a figure emerge from the shadows beyond the driveway and make its way gracefully across the yard. If I hadn't known, I could've guessed it was Bo by watching him move. He was like a light-footed predator, quick and sure.

He stopped a few feet from the window. The dusk-to-dawn light backlit his head, giving him a halo, but I could still see his face well enough to know that he watched me. My heart fluttered and my stomach clenched, squeezing tightly around the dozens of butterfly wings that moved inside it.

One slow step at a time, he made his way to the window. His nearly-black eyes never left mine until he was standing right in front of me, only a thin sheet of glass between our faces.

He said nothing, made no other move, simply stood watching me, and I him. While I waited, I drank him in, and, as always, I was stirred.

For the first time, I noticed that his glossy black hair had grown. It brushed the collar of his charcoal t-shirt. But other than that, he looked exactly the same as the first time I'd seen him: rock hard jaw cut from the palest of stone, straight nose, chiseled mouth, dark slashing brows. He was so handsome he took my breath away.

And his eyes. I couldn't count the number of times I'd gotten lost in their liquid depths, the number of times I'd wanted to. Over the last weeks, I could close my own eyes and picture his dark chocolate orbs with perfect clarity. They made me feel weak, just like they did now.

I raised the window and stepped back. Bo was in front of me in an instant, staring down at me wordlessly.

I shivered at his closeness, the embers of all that was between us leaping immediately to flame. But this time, the heat took a back seat to something troubling that I sensed in Bo, a sadness that seemed fresh and raw.

My brow furrowed. "What is it?"

Bo took the final step that would bring my body into contact with his and he drew me gently into his arms. Though I had no idea why, my heart felt like it was breaking.

"What is it?" I repeated, my voice muffled against the side of his neck.

Careful not to squeeze me too tightly, Bo held me as if he was a drowning man hanging on to dry land. It went a long way toward alarming me.

Still he said nothing.

And my concern mounted.

"Bo, please. Tell me what's wrong."

I felt as much as heard him sigh.

"I saw her."

My lungs seized inside my chest. Who? The girl that was bound to take my place at his side? The only girl in the world that I felt like I couldn't compete with?

"Who?" I asked, though I dreaded the answer.

"My mother."

I gasped.

"And?"

"She didn't even know me."

I closed my eyes against his pain. If a voice could bleed with a wound so deep, then Bo's was like an arterial spray. My heart cried out for him.

"Oh, Bo," I whispered, wishing there was something I could do or say, anything to ease the hurt. "I'm so sorry."

"I doubted you." It was a statement of fact. "I shouldn't have." And another. "I'm the one who should be sorry."

"I don't blame you. If I didn't think you needed to know, I wouldn't have told you. I would never hurt you like that on purpose."

"I know. And I love you for that."

It was wrong of me to feel so much pleasure at his words when he was in such agony. But I did.

Neither of us spoke for a long time. Bo simply held me, swaying gently back and forth. One of his hands stroked my hair, the other my back. And, while his touch sent chills racing down to my toes, the warmth of desire had succumb to a deep and abiding comfort born of love.

After several minutes had passed, Bo reached down and scooped me up in his arms and carried me to the bed, where he gently laid me down and dragged the covers up over me. Without a word, he stretched out beside me and pulled me back into his arms. With my head on his chest, his invincible heart beating beneath my ear and his strong hands holding me tight, I knew I'd never be happier, more at peace. I knew I'd never be more whole.

CHAPTER EIGHT

As far as Mondays go, it was probably one of the best I could remember. My day started with opening my eyes to see Bo standing over me. I must've heard him stir.

It was still dark outside, but I could see in the moonlight pouring through the window that he was starting to fade. I didn't know how long it had been since he fed.

He smiled down at me, a smile that said he was feeling a little bit better, and then he leaned over and kissed me.

"I'll see you later."

"Do you have to go?"

He nodded.

"I won't be far."

I blinked and he was gone. He'd already stolen out the window like a puff of cooling air.

For the rest of the morning, I carried a glow with me. It burned inside my chest, making me feel warm and fuzzy all over. Each time an unwelcome, disturbing thought sneaked into my mind, I'd bury it ruthlessly. I refused to let worry and insecurity over the inevitable ruin one more day.

By lunch, my glorious early hours had begun to lose some of their luster. It seemed that the high I got from being near Bo, the happiness and fulfillment that I felt in his presence, wasn't lasting me as long as it once had. It was as if I required more and more as time went on, like my need was growing by the minute.

People had been whispering all morning long, speculating about the fates of Summer, Aisha, Drew and Jason, the most recent disappearances. Most of the talk involved Jason and Summer since their altercation had not only been very violent, but witnessed as well.

Bailey wasn't at school to right the rumors, so people were making up all sorts of things to fill in the blanks. I'd even heard someone say that Summer had been winged. I nearly laughed out loud. Winged!

I was carrying my tray to the lunch table, observing the easy conversation and relaxed atmosphere as I approached. I sat in Drew's seat, not as a sign of disrespect, but because I didn't want to give even the appearance of taking Summer or Trinity's place as head nasty girl.

As I squeezed dressing onto my salad, I listened to the various conversations taking place around me. When a hush fell across the table, I looked up to identify the cause. I stopped mid-squeeze as Aisha let the cafeteria door close gently behind her.

Her normally-rich cocoa skin had an uncharacteristic pallor and her face was ashy in a way I hadn't noticed before. Her sparkling brown eyes were dull and haunted. She looked terrible. Whatever had happened to her had obviously taken its toll.

She made a bee line for me, giving all her well-wishers a nod of thanks and a small smile along the way. She sat down right next to me, just as she had sat next to Summer and Trinity before that.

Once she was seated, everyone clamored for her attention, firing question after question at her. For a girl who truly loved the spotlight, Aisha looked incredibly uncomfortable. I couldn't help the frown that pulled at my eyebrows.

"Maybe we should give her a minute to breathe, guys," I suggested, raising my voice just enough to be heard at our table. "We're all glad to have her back and I'm sure she'll tell us what happened when she's ready. Right, Aisha?" I said, looking at her meaningfully.

I could see the gratitude light her troubled eyes. "Yeah, but there's not much to tell. I can't remember a lot of what happened, so..."

She trailed off, effectively nipping any subsequent questions in the bud. If she had no memory, an interrogation was pointless.

Disappointment was evident on many faces. They could see that they weren't going to get a juicy story and they were deflated. It was ridiculous how much the people of my school lived, positively lived, for some good gossip. But, never fear. They'd have some spine-tingling, completely fictitious stories made up and ready to go by the end of the day. I felt sure at least a few of them would feature Aisha as some sort of caped super hero, too.

When conversation finally started back up all around the table, Aisha turned to me and smiled.

"Thanks, Ridley."

"No problem."

She looked at me expectantly, but I had no idea what to say to her. Like everyone else, all sorts of crazy explanations were flitting through my head. Unlike everyone else, however, I knew the scary kinds of things that were out there going bump in the night, things that were likely responsible for Aisha's woodland disappearance.

"So no one has seen Summer?" Aisha asked quietly.

I felt the frown again. It wasn't so much the question itself; it was the way she asked it, as if she knew something that we didn't.

"Well, did you hear about what happened at the dance?"

Aisha nodded.

"Yeah, well, that's the only time anyone's seen her since the bonfire in the woods Friday night."

Aisha nodded, glancing suspiciously around the table, as if to make sure no one else was listening.

"Since she left with you."

Aisha's eyes darted back to me and she watched me.

"You do remember," I whispered, careful to keep my expression casual so as not to alert anyone else to the seriousness of our conversation.

Again, Aisha looked surreptitiously around the neighboring faces. When she made her way back to me, she met my eyes and shrugged.

"Do you want to talk about it?"

"There's not much to tell really. I can't even be sure that it's real," she said, her voice quivering.

"What? What did you see?"

"It all seems like some kind of a weird dream. All these images and feelings…"

"Such as?" I prompted.

Aisha chewed her lip nervously as she searched for the words.

"Well, I remember going into the woods with Summer. She had to pee, but she didn't want to go by herself. You scared her that day at lunch, talking about the Slayer and stuff."

"Obviously not enough to cancel the party."

Aisha nodded. "That's the last thing that I remember clearly. Everything else just seems, I don't know, sort of fuzzy. Like a dream.

"For some reason, I thought I saw Trinity, but she didn't look like herself anymore. There was a lot of blood and I remember hurting and tasting something kind of rusty."

"And then what?"

"I remember looking up at the trees in the daylight. The sun was shining and it was so bright, but I could see the branches. I heard Summer crying and somebody whispering and then my legs started hurting."

Aisha paused, her haunted eyes scared and confused as she looked back over the last few days. I didn't rush her. I simply listened—carefully, anxiously. Full of dread.

"Then there were crickets and a really weird squealing sound. And laughter. But it was scary laughter. Crazy laughter. It sounded like Summer."

"Did you see her?"

"Well," Aisha paused again, uncertain. "I can't say for sure. I think I was still dreaming, because she was eating a-a—"

Aisha's chin started to tremble and her eyes filled with tears.

"What?"

"A pig, Ridley," she cried quietly. "She was on her knees in the leaves eating a pig raw. Like, she was taking big bites of it. There was blood everywhere and pieces of meat stuck to her face and—"

Aisha stopped, a gurgling sound bubbling in the back of her throat as bile crept up rebelliously. At her description, I could picture it as plainly as if I'd seen it myself. Saliva poured into my mouth.

"I know they were dreams, Ridley, but they felt so real. I can't get them out of my head." Tears left wet tracks down Aisha's ashen cheeks then dripped silently from her chin.

"How did you get home?"

"I don't know. My mom woke me up crying this morning. She was in the kitchen. I guess she'd been up all night. She was bawling about me drinking and staying over at a boy's house all weekend, but I had no idea what she was talking about. I told her I couldn't remember what had happened and she told me not to lie to her. She said I'd admitted it when I came home last night."

Aisha sniffled pitifully.

"But you don't remember talking to her?"

"No," she said emphatically. "I don't even remember coming home last night. She said it was, like, 2:00 in the morning. All I remember is the party on Friday, those weird dreams and waking up in my bed this morning. And I'm just so tired. There's no way I could've slept somewhere all weekend," she sobbed.

When she glanced around the table and saw that several pairs of eyes had turned toward her suspiciously, she wiped at her cheeks and pulled herself together somewhat.

"Aisha, have you noticed any marks on you? Bruises or scratches, cuts? Bites?" I added the last as nonchalantly as I could. She'd likely think I was talking about insect bites or animal bites rather than the type to which I was actually referring.

Aisha nodded. "I've got all sorts of places on me. It's like I rolled around in the woods or in a briar patch or something. There are marks everywhere."

"Nothing that particularly stands out, though?"

For the first time, Aisha eyed me suspiciously.

"What do you mean, Ridley?"

"I just thought maybe you got a tick or something. You know they say Lyme disease is dangerous. Makes you really sick."

Aisha's eyes rounded in surprise. "You know, I didn't even think of that."

I gave myself an imaginary pat on the back, congratulating myself for my quick thinking.

"I know, right?"

I felt satisfied when I saw the relief flood Aisha's eyes. I'd given her a plausible excuse for what she'd experienced, for the strange things she'd seen, as well as the time she'd missed. Until she found out definitively otherwise, she'd think she had a case of Lyme disease. But at least she wouldn't think she was crazy.

A healthy dose of guilt was lurking behind that fleeting sense of satisfaction, however, marring the momentary pleasure of it. I felt bad for lying to her. She'd likely been bitten by a vampire and then made to forget the whole experience. The holes in her memory were probably due to the vampire blood not being very mature, very potent. According to Bo and Lucius, there's much to be said for the power of the blood. That made an even stronger argument for the case that the offending vampire might be Trinity.

Trinity! How could I have forgotten her so easily? It was becoming painfully clear that she hadn't forgotten any of us. I wondered if that's what had happened to Summer. Had Trinity fed from her and made Summer lose her mind? Was

Summer so weak that she'd fall apart after only one bite? Or even two? Lucius said it was possible.

When I started to really think about it, Summer seemed exactly that weak. Personality-wise anyway. I had no idea what her actual constitution was like. Maybe Trinity had been feeding on her all this time. We'd probably never know.

And the worst part was that, if Trinity decided to attack any of the rest of us, there was nothing we could do about it. Other than destroying her heart, there was no defense against her, against vampires.

Except for Bo. He was our only weapon.

Bo could take care of Trinity. He was her equal. Not even that. He was her superior. Whatever was really going on with Bo, whoever he really was, he was strong. And special. There was no doubt about that.

Aisha and I sort of let the subject drop after that. I bent my head and plowed through my salad as she began engaging the people around her, evidently feeling much more secure in her sanity.

I could see life seeping back into her eyes a little at a time, though she still wasn't 100%. Something had happened to her—physically at the very least. Of that, I was sure. I could only hope that Bo would be able to do something to ensure that this kind of thing didn't happen to anyone else, and certainly not to Aisha again. I doubted she'd be able to withstand another attack and remain the Aisha that we all knew.

That afternoon, Aisha skipped practice, which didn't surprise me one bit. Even though there was the hint of a spark back in her eyes, she still didn't look like she could make it all the way through a single cheer.

After practice, I carried my duffel to my car. I found that I was dreading going home, but at the same time, I was also strangely anxious. I knew that it wasn't very likely that Bo would appear until after dark, especially if he had fed, which I could only assume that he had, considering his increasingly translucent state when he left my house. That's why, rather than sitting around and watching the minutes tick by at home, I decided to visit Savannah.

The one good thing about her being blind, the condition I thought just might save her life, was that she was rarely, if ever, alone. During the day, she was with her tutor. Nights and evenings, she was with her dad. I doubted that anyone would be stupid enough to attack her when she wasn't alone. At least, I hoped that was the case. Of course, if this was Trinity we were talking about...

When I rang the bell, Mr. Grant came to the door. He was wiping his hands, which made me want to kick myself for my second blatant show of inconsideration. It was near supper time and he was probably cooking. Again.

I started apologizing as soon as he opened the screen. "I'm so sorry, Mr. Grant. I've come at a bad time again. And without calling, too." I cringed. "I'm sorry. I'll stop by to see Savannah another time."

"Don't be silly," he said with a dismissive wave of his hand. "She's in her room. Come on in."

The strong scents of Italian food smacked me in the face as soon as I stepped into the foyer.

"Mmm, something smells amazing." For a moment, I felt a pang of envy, wishing that I came home every day to a house that smelled like spaghetti and a parent that actually cooked.

"Lasagna," he said with a broad smile. "Secret family recipe. You ought to stay and eat with us."

"Thank you, but I shouldn't."

"You know, you're going to have to take me up on dinner one of these days, right?"

"I will."

"I'm a gourmet chef. You just don't know what you're missing."

I grinned. Somehow I thought Mr. Grant might be prone to exaggeration.

"Dad, leave her alone. She didn't come to be pressured into food poisoning."

"Listen to Miss Smarty Pants back there, ruling from her throne," he teased. "Just because you don't know how to appreciate food doesn't mean I'm not a gourmet chef. And I haven't given anybody food poisoning in years," he said, winking at me.

"Ridley, walk away. Right now. Just turn left and walk away."

Mr. Grant chuckled and tipped his head, indicating that I should proceed to Savannah's room.

As I approached the hallway, I saw that the ball-of-fur dog that Savannah had named after a feline was crashed on his side, right in my way.

"Hi, Kitty," I said, bending down to scratch the dog behind its ears. He closed his eyes and grunted. "Oh, that feels good, huh?"

He grunted again, as if in agreement.

I straightened, stepped over him and continued my path on to Savannah's room, chuckling all the way at a dog named "Kitty."

"You saved me!" Savannah sighed dramatically when I stepped into her bright room. "He's driving me insane."

I had no doubt she was referring to her dad.

"Oh, yeah. It must be terrible to have a dad who loves you to distraction and cooks you dinner every night."

"But he-he—" She growled, tripping over her words. "You don't... I-I." Savannah finally stopped trying to stammer her way through reasons she didn't like her awesome dad. With a sigh, she rolled her eyes. "Eh, you're right. He's pretty cool."

"Much better," I said as I sat down on the end of her bed. "So, wha'cha been up to?"

"You mean besides driving a bus full of kindergartners around town and practicing my blindfold-less knife-throwing act for the circus?"

"Of course."

"Not much," she admitted. "How was school? Give me the goods," she demanded, pulling her legs under her and getting comfortable for a dump truck load of gossip.

"Believe it or not, there's not much to tell. No one knows what happened to Drew. Summer's wanted for questioning and Aisha turned up at school. Unless, of course, you listen to the rumor mill. According to those reports, Summer is a winged creature and Drew joined a rock band and is currently touring the lower forty-nine."

Savannah barely batted an eye. "And Jason?"

"Oh, I forgot about Jason. He's the one the winged Summer flew off with."

"Naturally."

I had to grin.

"And Aisha? What's her deal?"

I snorted for effect. "She has no clue where she was all weekend. Must've been some kind of bender."

Only I knew that it wasn't. I couldn't very well tell her what Aisha had told me, though. Besides, what I really wanted to talk about had nothing to do with Aisha. Or the other three for that matter.

"So, how have you been? Seen anything strange lately?"

Savannah's face tightened noticeably and she got up to close her bedroom door.

"I know it sounds insane, but I also know what I saw."

"I didn't say you sounded insane."

"You didn't have to."

True. I thought she was imagining things and she knew that's what I thought. But somewhere in the back of my mind, when I put it in the context of all the crazy things I'd seen in the last few months, it didn't seem so farfetched anymore.

"Alright, it sounds crazy, but I believe you, whether you think I do or not."

Savannah softened.

"Believe me, I wondered about it myself when I first saw him standing there. But then, when he spoke and then he touched me..."

As I listened to Savannah, I found myself sympathizing with her, with her need to believe that Devon hadn't left her, that he was back, that he was...

I grabbed Savannah's hand, feeling a sudden urgency come over me.

"At the dance, you said Devon was going to see you later. Did he?"

Savannah's face fell a bit.

"No. I haven't seen him since."

I could tell that admitting that came at a great cost, the cost of some of her faith in what she believed she saw.

"Well, things happen. You know how it is. Plans change."

She nodded, but I could see that it really didn't make her feel any better.

"I know what I saw, Ridley." Her voice was quiet and her eyes were sad as she looked in my general direction, unseeing. "I know it was him. I know it."

It sounded like she was trying to convince herself she'd seen Devon as much as me. My heart wrenched for her.

"Could you see anything else when you saw him? I mean, describe it. Describe what you saw."

Savannah's face lit up as she thought about it.

"It was amazing. I was dancing with Zach and the entire world was dark all around me, just like it has been since the accident. But then I saw this blurry light spot near the double doors. I blinked a few times, but it didn't go away. I watched it move around the back wall of the gym, almost like it was circling us or maybe even like it was circling me."

Savannah laughed.

"For a second, I thought maybe I was dying. Isn't that stupid?" she asked.

I laughed, too, even though I didn't think anything about her story was funny. If anything, it was getting scarier by the minute.

"I would never admit this to anybody else, but since I lost my sight, I've thought a lot about death. There have been more than a few times that I've even prayed for it."

"Savan—"

"I know, I know," she said, holding up her hand to stop me. "I'm fine now. It's just been...hard."

"But that's what we're—"

"Anyway," she interrupted pointedly right before she cleared her throat and continued, obviously not interested in pursuing that subject. "I watched it move over toward the other door, the one that leads back out into the hall in front of the bathrooms. I thought it was waiting to take me to heaven. Assuming that God would even want a dork like me up there with Him," she said self-deprecatingly.

"Savannah," I began, but she shushed me.

"So, when the song was over, I made my excuses to Zach and I followed it out the door and down the hall to the bathroom."

Savannah started to smile—a huge, gleeful spread of the lips that brought out her dimples and made her eyes sparkle.

"As soon as I stepped through the door, I could see him. I couldn't see anything else. Everything else was black, just like always. But I could see him, plain as day, and that's all that matters."

"What did he look like?"

"Heavenly. Gorgeous. Just like always," she said as she sighed adoringly. But then, she wrinkled her brow a tiny bit and pursed her lips. "Well, maybe he looked a little different, not exactly like he did. But maybe that's just because it's been so long since I've seen anything that nothing would look the same to me now."

"Different? Different how?"

She tilted her head to one side in thought. "Um, he seemed maybe a little paler and his eyes might've looked a little different, too."

"Like how?"

"I don't know. Lighter maybe, but also less...carefree or something, like he was carrying the weight of the world on his shoulders."

"And he told you not to tell anyone, right?"

"Yeah."

"Did he say why?"

"Nope. And I don't need to know. He trusted me and I don't intend to disappoint him."

I tried to choose my words carefully.

"Savannah, what if he's in some kind of trouble?"

I saw the shadow of doubt cross her face, but then she shook it away.

"The only thing he asked me to do was to keep him a secret, so that's what I'm going to do. Period."

I knew by the stubborn tilt of her chin that I wasn't going to get her to change her mind. The best I could hope for was to influence future visits.

"When you see him next time, would you do me a favor? Would you ask him to come and see me?"

She hesitated.

"Look, if he knows anything about what might've happened to Bo, then I want to know. Surely you can understand that."

Though terribly unfair, I pulled the Bo card, knowing it would get to her. She knew how it felt to have someone you love disappear without a trace. She also knew how it felt to have them return to you. Savannah was too kindhearted to begrudge me that if she could help it.

"Alright, but I can't make any promises. He's probably going to be mad that I told you anyway."

"You had no choice. I nearly ran into him in the bathroom, remember? He doesn't have to know that I didn't see him, too."

I quickly turned the conversation to less upsetting things to keep it light during the last half of my visit. When Mr. Grant came and knocked on Savannah's door, I figured it was probably time for the normal people to eat, which meant I needed to leave.

Savannah walked down the hall with me, but when we got to the end, I told her, "I can see myself out. You go eat."

"Are you sure you can make it all the way over there without the help of a blind girl?" She was referring to the front door that was all of fifteen feet away

"I think I can handle it."

"If you're sure…"

"Go eat, goofy."

Savannah grinned and headed into the kitchen.

"Ridley," Mr. Grant called before I'd even taken my second step.

"Sir?"

"Why don't you come for dinner Wednesday night? We're having tacos. Surely I can't screw up a taco."

Savannah coughed pointedly and I had to smile.

"Come on, Ridley. Put the poor guy out of his misery. Maybe he'll quit trying to be a chef if he hears the sounds of someone besides me puking after dinner."

"Well, since it's for a good cause," I said, agreeing.

"Alright. We'll eat at 6:00. Come as early as you want. Maybe you can keep this one from sulking," he said, tipping his head toward Savannah, who then stuck her tongue out at him. Or at least in his general direction.

"I can try."

Savannah turned and stuck her tongue out at me, too.

On the short drive home, I pondered Savannah. And Devon. I couldn't help but wonder what Savannah was seeing. Was he just a figment of her imagination? A manifestation of her intense desire not only to see again, but to see Devon again as well? Could she be seeing a ghost or some other type of otherworldly being? Or, was it possible that Devon was a vampire and Savannah was somehow seeing him?

Leaving my right hand on the steering wheel, I rubbed at my throbbing temple with the fingertips of my other. Too many questions, not nearly enough answers.

I pulled into the driveway, leaving plenty of room for Mom to slide her car in beside mine, and turned off the engine. The house was dark and empty and I thought of Savannah's warm home with longing. Maybe I should've stayed for dinner.

"Too late now," I said to the empty car as I opened the door to get out.

Inside, I put my things away, changed clothes and went to the kitchen to make myself a sandwich. I took the plain ham and cheese back to my room to munch on while I read over some Chemistry notes for an upcoming test. As I bit into the cold meat, I thought again of Savannah's family. Even though it was just her and her dad, there was so much more normalcy there. I felt guilty for the wave of envy that washed over me.

A while later, when I'd become firmly ensconced in the amalgamation of gold and mercury, I heard a noise at my window. My stomach lurched in response. I'd been so absorbed in my homework that Bo had managed to sneak up on me, which wasn't easy considering that my body seemed to continually search the environment for any sign of him, for any indication that he might be near.

I slid excitedly off the bed and hurried to the window and threw it open. By the time I realized my mistake, it was too late. Someone was already standing inside my room, only it wasn't Bo.

CHAPTER NINE

My heart was slamming around inside my chest like a pinball gone wild. My breath shuddered in and out through my trembling lips. My mind scurried frantically over a thousand less-than-helpful things.

"Drew."

Even if he hadn't gotten into my room so fast that I could barely track him, I would've known he was a vampire. He was different. I could feel it. I could smell it, too. He reeked of pine, something I'd never smelled on him before tonight.

If none of my other senses had worked, though, I would've been able to see the changes. His skin was ghostly white with a dark webbing of veins visible underneath and his lips were ruby red, looking almost stained. I realized with a start that there was blood on them. And it appeared to be fresh.

My stomach roiled with nausea and I looked up to meet his pale, milky-green eyes. They were trained on me and they looked ravenous.

My one coherent thought was that he couldn't have been the one to attack me in the woods the night of the bonfire. Drew must've been turned sometime later. The question was: by whom?

"Well, well, well. If it isn't the cheater," he said in a low voice as he approached me.

I hated myself for stumbling backwards, but I did. I couldn't stand the thought of him being anywhere near me.

"What do you want, Drew?"

"What do you think I want, T?"

The use of his pet name for me reminded me that this was, in fact, the guy for whom I had once harbored a true affection. Though that thought gave me a bit more compassion for him, it did little to put me at ease. There was something in his face that said he was here to take what he wanted, whatever he wanted.

"It doesn't matter, because you're not staying." I took another step away from him.

"And I suppose that you're going to make me leave. Is that it?"

He advanced two steps, bringing me within his long arms' reach.

"I shouldn't have to, Drew. You're not this guy. Come on."

"What if I am? I thought you liked 'this guy'?"

"I liked you just the way you were."

"Just not enough."

"I can't help the way I feel, Drew."

"Well, neither can I," he said softly, reaching out to twirl a lock of my hair around his finger. "Did you ever want me, T?"

His eerie pale eyes were focused on the curl that he held, but there was something about the way he asked the question that gave me a rush of fear.

"Drew, I-I. You know I- when we—"

"You were always a terrible liar, T," he said. And when his eyes met mine again, I had one instant of warning before he grabbed me. Not that it mattered; he was a hundred times faster than me. There was no way I could have avoided him.

Steely fingers wrapped around my upper arms, squeezing so tight I thought my bones would snap. I gasped in pain just as Drew's lips smothered mine.

He forced his tongue through my half-parted lips, bringing with it the metallic taste of blood. I used mine to try and push it back out, but he was very forceful. I raised my hands to push at his chest, but it was like trying to move a two-ton boulder. He didn't budge. He was stronger than anyone, anything I'd ever encountered. Even though I was sure Bo was stronger, he had never tried to force himself on me.

One hand let go of my arm to palm the back of my head, tilting it slightly so that he could deepen the kiss. I couldn't pull away; he held my face snugly to his.

I made noises of objection in my throat, noises he completely disregarded. It wasn't until I felt his other hand at my breast that I really started to panic.

I slapped at it, but it was no use. He was so incredibly strong that I felt like a child struggling to fight him off.

Something sharp grazed my lip and I tasted warm, fresh blood. Mine. That's when Drew's reaction, and his intention, changed.

A low growl started in the back of his throat and his mouth left mine. He lifted his head briefly so that he could look down into my eyes. I had to wonder why, but when I saw his face, I knew. He wanted me to see him—to see what he'd become, to see what he was going to do, to see what my fate was going to be. He wanted me to see it coming.

His lips curled back from his four razor sharp canines in a devilish sneer. He didn't bother to hide the delight, the malicious pleasure he was feeling. He had no qualms about taking anything he wanted from me whether I wanted to give it or not.

I closed my eyes against the unavoidable, wishing that I had the strength to fend him off, or that Bo would somehow choose this very minute to come to my window. But when I felt Drew's lips at my neck and the sharp pinch of his teeth, I knew that no one was going to save me. I was going to die all alone at the hands of a spiteful ex-boyfriend who'd become a monster.

As I was staring down the sullen face of inevitability, a thought occurred to me. It was both promising and troubling. I remembered Bo telling me that the young vampires couldn't control their venom as well as the older ones. What if he failed to kill me dead? What if Drew accidentally turned me?

I wasn't sure that I wanted to be a vampire. I mean, the thought of spending eternity with Bo was euphoric, even if it entailed being trapped inside a traitorous body that was possessed of an unquenchable thirst for blood. But what would I do when Bo found his true mate, the one who was destined to save him? I'd be stuck with that misery forever. Sometimes I wondered if I could make it through lunch without Bo. How could I manage that pain forever?

My rising panic triggered a surge of adrenaline and an insanely frantic need to get away. It was that adrenaline that gave my arms a little extra oomph when I pushed against

Drew's chest in a last-ditch effort to regain freedom. It was just enough to force Drew back a tad and dislodge his teeth from my neck, albeit painfully. It felt as though he tore out a big chunk of flesh when he stumbled back.

At first, I think Drew was surprised. Actually, I was, too. I hadn't really expected to be able to move him at all. Thankfully, I'd caught him off guard.

We stood facing each other for only a fraction of a second, though it felt much longer, as if time had somehow been suspended.

I bolted for the door, but Drew was already grabbing me and hauling me back against his chest. I could see our reflection in the mirror, me facing it and him standing behind me. I saw the hunk of flesh hanging down beneath my ear, flesh he'd torn away when I'd moved. Blood had soaked my sweatshirt on one side and the sheer amount caused me a bit of alarm.

I kept thinking I need to put pressure on that. I need to put pressure on that. But then I looked up at Drew's face and my mind instantly and sharply focused on him.

I saw the anger in his expression, something close to blind rage. I saw hunger as well, a hunger that I knew wouldn't be satisfied until he'd drained me dry.

All other thoughts abandoned me as I watched him bare his teeth and drive them into the other side of my neck. I wanted to struggle, but he held me so tightly, I couldn't.

I tried to kick back at him, but he didn't even appear to feel it. I started to scream once, but he only lifted his head and bit down harder in a different spot, eliciting a gasp that pulled my scream right out of the air.

My heart was beating so fast it felt like nothing more than a quick flutter in my chest. It was getting harder and harder to stand in Drew's arms. I found myself relying less on my legs to support me and more on his vise grip.

An annoying buzz started to ring in my ears, becoming louder and louder as my vision began to swim. I heard noises off in the distance, so far away that they had to be at the neighbor's house. Strangely, though, they seemed to coincide with things taking place in my room.

In the mirror, I saw Bo literally jump through the window behind us. I felt like smiling, but I couldn't muster one. At the moment, I was having trouble just keeping my lids open.

When he straightened, his face contorted into a stricken mask of fear and rage. I heard a voice say, You're killing her, and though the voice was unmistakably Bo's and it matched the movement of his glorious lips, it sounded too far away to be happening so close to me.

Right before my eyes, Bo's face transformed into the monster I'd first thought him to be. His milky eyes matched Drew's and he roared, baring four glittering fangs. His face and neck were covered with veins clearly visible beneath his uber pale skin, veins pulsing with a need that I couldn't fathom.

I knew that Bo's need wasn't just his normal physical requirement of blood. This was a need for the blood of reckoning, blood that would come from Drew and could end up costing him his life.

Drew's face registered no change at first, but then when Bo came for him, he seemed to snap out of the hunger that had been driving him. A fraction of a second before Bo reached him, Drew lifted his head and his opaque green eyes met mine in the mirror. In them, I saw shock.

Bo grabbed him by the throat and lofted him high into the air, where Drew dangled impotently. Drew struggled, but he couldn't move Bo. Drew brought his hands down to

Bo's wrist, trying to loosen Bo's fingers, to pry them away from his neck, but his efforts made no impact. Drew raised his legs and kicked at Bo's chest. Bo's flinch was nearly imperceptible.

Like tossing a small boy, Bo threw Drew up against the wall beside my bed and then rushed forward in attack, burying his teeth deep in the soft tissue of Drew's neck. Drew leaned helplessly against the wall, stunned and unable to move inside the iron grip of Bo's arms.

"Bo, no," I mumbled, unable to garner the strength to shout.

Drew's eyes dropped to mine where I sat crumpled in the floor with barely enough energy to remain upright. As I watched, the shock drifted away from his now-blue eyes, replaced by the passive tides of resignation. But there was something else there, too, something that looked an awful lot like regret.

"Bo, don't." I tried again, but I was just too weak.

I didn't think Bo heard me, but when he lifted his head and turned to look at me, I knew he had. I could see the blood lust all over his face. I'd seen that look before. It was a thirst for revenge, and last time, it had nearly killed him.

As Bo and I stared at each other, a quiet voice pierced the stillness.

"Kill me," it said.

It was Drew.

Bo and I both looked to him, but Drew was watching only me.

"Let him kill me, T," he said pitifully. "I can't live like this."

Each word stabbed at my heart.

"You can't mean that," I whispered. This was the Drew I knew. This was the Drew that I once thought I loved. It was there, in his eyes, on his face. He was sincere. And he was miserable.

"I do." He turned his eyes to Bo. "Do it," he encouraged. When Bo didn't make a move, Drew gritted his teeth and spat, "Do it!"

Bo looked to me and I shook my head, hoping he wasn't considering honoring Drew's request. He dropped his eyes from mine before sliding them back to Drew.

"Bo, you're not—"

I didn't even get the words out before Bo disappeared out the window with Drew in tow. He handled him like a rag doll, like Drew wasn't an incredibly strong vampire himself. Bo was just so much more powerful, more powerful than even I'd known.

I knew I didn't have enough juice to make it to the window, much less outside to follow them, so I lay over on my side and held a hand as tightly as possible over the gaping hole in my neck.

I felt the slow pump of blood oozing between my fingers. I couldn't press hard enough to make it stop. And I was so tired, much too tired to keep holding on.

As the light began to fade from my view, I was thankful that Drew hadn't managed to turn me. Not that I wanted to die, but I thought becoming a vampire destined to live eternity in mourning and heartache was the less desirable outcome.

I closed my eyes, the cold from the floor seeping into every cell of my body as I lay there, waiting to die. I heard noises again, still far away. I managed to open my eyes just long enough to see Bo striding toward me. Quickly, he bent and scooped me up.

At that moment, I felt complete, like all was right with the world. I would die in Bo's strong arms, with his tangy scent in my nostrils and the image of his once-again fully human face burned onto the backs of my eyes. There was nothing else I could've asked for, unless it would have been for more time.

He carried me to the bed and tore open his wrist, holding it to my mouth.

"Take it, Ridley," he said softly. "You need blood to heal."

"I can't be a vampire," I managed. "I don't want to-to..." I stammered. I was just so, so weak.

When my lids fluttered open once more, I saw an expression of hurt and worry on Bo's face. I wasn't sure why it was there, but I wished for it to ease. He was too beautiful to feel pain, or at least that's the way it should be.

Bending his muscular arms and curling me up to his mouth, I felt Bo's tongue as he tasted the blood at my throat. When he lowered me, I saw that his eyes had already begun to pale again at just that small taste.

"Finish it. I'd rather you do it."

"Ridley, if there's any venom in your blood, it's not much. Not enough to turn you. Take my blood. I can't lose you, too," he said quietly, his eyes closing briefly, as if in pain. "Please don't do this to me."

He held his dripping wrist to my mouth once more and I opened, wrapping my lips around his warm skin, suckling his sticky sweet blood until that familiar need to sleep stole over me.

****

Of all the terrible ways to wake up from such an emotionally and physically traumatic experience, my mother's drunken screeching was probably one of the worst.

"Ridley, why didn't you do something?"

Mom's harsh, slurred words penetrated the thick soup that had invested my head. I battled through it until I managed to crack my eyelids and look around the lamp-lit cavern of my bedroom.

Memories of what had happened rushed in quickly and I sat up, searching the shadows for Bo. My nose, now even more sensitive to his scent since drinking his blood, detected hints of him lingering in the air around me. My ears prickled with the sounds of someone moving lightly across the grass in the front yard, just past my still-open window. But more than what my five senses could detect was the sharp visceral knowledge that he'd just left, that he wasn't yet very far from me. That tie to him, that bond to his body, his soul, his presence, was once again firmly and strongly intact.

I took a moment to savor it, closing my eyes and relishing the way his blood sang in my veins, hummed along my nerves. I could almost feel him behind my eyes.

But then something unpleasant jolted me out of my introverted musings.

"Ridley, answer me!"

With a sigh and a roll of my eyes, I scooted off the bed and opened the door. It wasn't until I was halfway out into the hall that I remembered what I must look like, all covered in blood. I knew that my marks would be healed for the most part, courtesy of Bo's amazingly powerful blood. But his blood couldn't shout out stains like good ol' detergent could.

Glancing down at my sweatshirt, I was surprised to see that I wasn't wearing a sweatshirt at all. And the yoga pants I'd put on were gone as well. I backed up and hurried into the bathroom for a quick peek.

My neck was a bit red and it looked like it had been scratched more than anything, but the blood had been carefully wiped away. I parted the neck of the men's button-up flannel shirt I was now wearing and saw that even my chest was clean, free of the rivulets of blood that had gushed from my torn throat.

Heat erupted and spread across my chest and down my arms, making my nipples tighten and tingle. Bo had changed my clothes and cleaned me up, and even now, just thinking about him touching me, taking my clothes off and replacing them with clean ones, made my body warm as if I could still feel his gentle hands on me.

In the mirror, I could see that my pupils were dilated and my lips were slightly parted with want. An ache started at my core and radiated through me, and I bit my lip to keep from moaning. With my enhanced connection to Bo, sometimes my intense physical attraction to him could be a bit of a bother, especially at times like this when my mother was apparently on a drunken rampage. I took a deep, clarifying breath to compose myself before heading out to face her.

When I found her, she was leaning up against the coat closet just inside the front door, working hard at undoing the strap around her ankle that held her shoe in place. I watched as she struggled to remain upright, wrestling with it while she balanced on one high heel-shod foot. I doubted she could do that stone cold sober, much less this deep in her cups.

Finally, with a frustrated growl, she slid down to the floor and brought her foot up closer so that she could work at the buckle.

"Need some help?" I asked, having seen her fight with it long enough.

Mom looked up, glaring at me from under her mussed bangs. "Not from you," she said hatefully.

"What's the matter, Mom?"

"The same thing that's always the matter, Ridley. You let Izzy die and I don't think I can ever forgive you for that."

I'd heard this a few times before. Occasionally, Mom would get a hold of a nasty mood and, when coupled with vodka by the gallon, she would tell me where she really felt the blame for Izzy's death lay—with me.

Regardless, though, it was always an excruciating slap in the face to know that anyone would dare blame me for the death of the sister that I loved so much. I'd gladly have taken Izzy's place—many times I'd wished it had been me instead—but that wasn't an option. She was practically dead as soon as the car struck the tree. From the second we'd hit, Izzy's fate had been out of my control.

But that would never be enough for Mom. She would mourn the loss of the "good daughter" for the rest of her life. That, in turn, meant that she'd always point the finger of blame at the survivor—me.

It aggravated me when I felt tears collect behind my lashes.

"I didn't let Izzy die, Mom," I said, my voice betraying me with a tremble.

"You did! It should've been you, not her," she spat angrily, tearing at the strap that crossed her ankle.

I bent to help her loosen the buckle.

"I wish it had been, Mom," I said quietly, sniffing softly, hoping that my distress would remain undetected.

Mom grabbed my chin and jerked my face up, our eyes meeting.

"Don't you dare try to make me feel guilty with your tears. You can't fool me. She would never have been on that road if it weren't for you. You don't deserve to cry for her."

"Mom, please. You know I would never hurt Izzy. I'd give anything to have her back."

"Hush," she said, turning her face from me. "I can't stand to hear it anymore. Just get that shoe off and leave me be."

Again, my body betrayed me. As I nimbly worked the shoe loose and away from Mom's foot, my tears peppered the tile of the foyer floor. I stood and handed her the shoe I'd just removed.

She took it from me, flinging it angrily down the hall toward her bedroom.

"Get out of my sight!"

Without so much as another glance in her direction, I turned and walked back to my room. When I closed the door behind me, I leaned back against it, hating the pain that suffused my chest. It was bad enough that I'd lost my sister almost four years ago, but in a way, I'd lost my entire family that fateful night, too.

My mother had drowned, first in her tears, then in her bitterness, now in her alcohol. And my father, he'd run away. Though he'd never really left home, left us, he was long gone, all the time, even when he was present on the weekends. He was just a shell of the man he used to be.

At least they can still manage to pretend some of the time, I told myself consolingly. I thought of my new curfew, of how I'd been restricted from being out by myself after dark. Even though it was an inconvenience, in a perverse way, I cherished the limitation. It was a reminder of what life used to be like when they cared, what life was probably like for other kids whose parents were actually present and accounted for, emotionally anyway.

Pushing away from the door, I reminded myself that I would only have to deal with it for a little while longer, until I graduated and was forced to figure out what to do with about my future since my lifelong plans were basically a shambles. But I'd think of something. I had to.

Feeling suddenly lost and melancholy, I switched off my lamp and curled up on my comforter, listening to the louder-than-normal night life that was singing outside my window. I fell asleep almost immediately, still exhausted and lethargic from my earlier tussle with Drew.

My eyes snapped open and the red clock numbers read 2:17. I was still curled up on my right side, facing the window, as the mattress dipped behind me. A cool hand slid over my hip, splaying across the skin of my belly where my flannel shirt lay parted.

I snuggled back into Bo. I didn't need to turn around and look. For one thing, I knew from his body temperature that I wouldn't be able to see him. He was freezing. I knew exactly who it was, though. Every cell in my body welcomed his closeness, all my senses opened up to take him in, like flower petals opening up for the sweet, wet kiss of the rain.

His cool lips grazed my neck, sending chill bumps down my left arm.

"It wasn't your fault," he whispered against my skin.

My heart squeezed and my throat constricted with emotion. I didn't have to ask what he meant. I knew. As I'd suspected, he hadn't been gone very long when I'd awakened and he must have been close enough to hear my mother's vicious barbs.

Tears burned my eyes as the pain of her comments came back in a flood. That's why I put them out of my mind. It hurt too bad to think about them.

"I know," I said quietly. "But it still hurts."

"I know," he said.

A single tear somehow managed to escape my tightly squeezed lids. Immediately, the cool air began to dry the wet trail it left on my cheek. When I felt composed enough to speak, I asked, "Drew?"

"Shh. We'll talk tomorrow."

Though I wanted to know, I didn't think I could handle one more thing on that night. Silently, I reached down and brought Bo's fingers to my lips. His hands were so strong, so capable, but I knew that there were some things in life that even Bo couldn't fix.

****

The next morning, Bo was already gone when my alarm went off. I hadn't even been aware of him leaving. In fact, I hadn't been aware of much of anything after I fell asleep in his arms.

I reached out to the place beside me, the place where he'd lain. The comforter was icy where his body had been. He couldn't have been gone very long.

Rolling over, I buried my face in the covers. They still smelled of him and, as always, my body reacted instantaneously with an ache that was becoming a part of my genetic makeup.

Thoughts of his sweet tenderness, his amazing ability to comfort me without saying a word brought me back to the myriad reasons for my distress. My mother, Izzy, Drew, Summer and Aisha, Trinity, some nebulous girl that floated out there on the horizon, waiting for the perfect moment to tear my life apart—all of it started buzzing around inside my head at once.

With a renewed determination that was matched only by the vampire blood-induced energy that I felt infusing my muscles, I pushed back the covers and hopped out of bed. I was going to take a hot shower and I wasn't coming out until all the bloody residue from last night's drama had been washed away, as well as all the negativity that seemed to permeate my entire life. Whatever the future held, I was going to enjoy the present. I was going to live and love like there was no tomorrow. For all I knew, that might be the case. At the rate I was going, on any given day there was a distinct possibility that tomorrow might never come.

Having the essence of Bo pouring through my veins seemed to help everything, that or it simply altered my perspective enough to view things differently. Even though I couldn't see him or necessarily feel him in that way I did when he was near, I felt like I carried him—or some part of him—with me all the time, as if he was with me at every turn, for every step.

When I got to school, I expected the majority of the talk to be about the recent disappearances and the even more recent attacks, as they had been every day for weeks. But today, the buzz was a bit different.

I heard snippets of conversations about the death of an elderly woman in neighboring Sumter. I was puzzled as to why that would be noteworthy at our high school, but I thought little of it. I knew that if there was even a scintilla of a juicy story there, it would be discussed at our lunch table *ad nauseum*.

I didn't have to wait that long to find out, though. Mrs. Dingle was already on it.

Perched atop her desk, the petite middle-aged woman pushed her frameless glasses up her not unattractive nose and flicked the paper open in front of her. When she began to read, I knew that she, too, had found the story something of an interest.

Sixty-one year old Maggie Jenner was found dead in her second floor apartment early yesterday morning. Jenner, reportedly attacked in her own bed, was brutally mauled and dismembered. Police originally suspected that Jenner was the victim of an animal attack, but after further investigation, authorities discovered that Jenner's apartment door was locked from the inside and her windows were inaccessible from the ground, suggesting that she was the victim of foul play. Though an animal attack has been officially ruled out, police have yet to name any suspects in connection with Jenner's untimely death. Lead Homicide Detective Alan Forbes was interviewed on site. He made a brief statement, only to say that police are following several possible avenues in relation to the case.

As Mrs. Dingle was reading, I kept thinking that the victim's name sounded familiar somehow, but I just couldn't place it. She quickly moved on to another story and then the bell rang, so it was easy to put the question out of my mind for the time being.

I coasted through the day, distracted and, strangely, a little happy. Lunch dampened my spirits a bit, though. I sat in Drew's seat again, only today I couldn't help but wonder what had happened to him. It made me queasy to think about Drew being miserable enough to want to die and Bo possibly giving in to the urge to kill him, whether Drew wanted and deserved it or not. As much as Drew and I had butted heads since our breakup, I still didn't want to see anything bad happen to him, anything worse than vampirism, that is.

Bo did pretty well with his condition, so I didn't think it was the worst possible fate. But apparently Drew disagreed. It made me wonder if there was more to it than what I'd originally thought.

Thinking about that was like unwrapping a gag gift. I was much more comfortable when vampirism was glamorized. I didn't want to think of it as being such a torturous existence that someone would want to die because of it.

My angst and growing disillusionment over vampires was only reinforced when Aisha didn't show up at our table. I hadn't seen her all day, which wasn't entirely unusual, but no one else had either, and that was out of the ordinary. She had an unmistakable way of being recognized, seen and heard wherever she went. She was very much like Trinity in that way.

I managed to shake off most of my funk by the time lunch was over, and my spirits were bolstered when I saw Aisha making her way across the field for practice. I ran out to meet her.

She looked a little worse than she had the day before, and I couldn't help but wonder what was going on with her. Lately, my suspicions ran toward vicious supernatural causes for nearly everything. Nothing was just an accident or bad luck anymore. I suspected vampires were at the root of everything from black eyes to pale skin to bad moods.

"Hey. Missed you at lunch today," I said lightly, falling into step beside her.

"Uh, I overslept so I just waited until after lunch to check in."

Aisha seemed to be going out of her way to avoid eye contact. I bent my head and engaged her on purpose.

"Is everything alright? Did you remember something else?"

"I'm fine," she said, meeting my eyes quickly then looking away.

I stopped. "Aisha, if something's wrong, you need to tell me. Maybe I can help you."

"Nothing's wrong." She tried to sound sincere, but I wasn't convinced.

"I can tell something's up, and you can talk to me. You can tell me anything and it will stay between us."

"There's nothing to talk about, Ridley. Seriously."

"You don't have to pretend with me, Aisha."

"I'm not pretending," she said, laughing nervously.

"Seriously, I might know—"

"Ridley!" she snapped. "Drop it. There's nothing you can do to help me. Now just let it go."

She stormed off and I stood rooted to my spot in the grass, watching her go. Now I knew something was up, but I had no way of finding out what it was if she didn't trust me enough to tell me, if she wouldn't talk to me.

Aisha walked right up to the group and started chatting, but I knew her well enough to know that she wasn't herself. She was less animated, less energetic and she just didn't look good. But obviously, she wasn't ready to tell me anything.

I made up my mind right then that I would just have to convince her that she could trust me, that I could and would help her.

I jogged back and started practice.

As we worked through a new cheer, I traded hats between captain and stand-in base cheerleader. Since Trinity and Summer were both gone, we had to make some adjustments, which put me into the mix in a totally different way.

The last part of our new cheer included some simple shoulder stands. Even though I wasn't really the size that bases usually were, I moved one of the smaller girls over to pair with me so that we could make it work. As a couple, we were next to Aisha and her partner.

As we were moving through the second rehearsal of the cheer, Aisha faltered on her climb and fell from Mia's shoulders. She landed with a dull thud on the ground and lay there for a few seconds, addled and breathless.

Being the closest to her, I was one of the first of us to come to her rescue.

"Are you ok?"

Aisha nodded her head, dazed.

"Can you sit up?"

Again, she nodded.

I reached behind her to help her into a sitting position and, as her splayed legs came together, I noticed a mark on the inside of her right thigh. It looked like a bite mark.

Not meaning to, I paused when I saw it. Aisha saw me staring and quickly straightened her shorts, effectively covering the wound, hiding it from my knowing eyes.

She looked at me for several seconds, and I at her, neither of us speaking. I knew then that she had remembered something—something important, something scary. Something she was afraid to tell anyone else.

I didn't doubt her sincerity when she'd told me yesterday that she couldn't remember anything. Her tears were too real, her distress too genuine. But now, I could tell that she was lying to me. I could also tell that she was afraid.

With a meaningful look in her eye and a firm shake of her head, Aisha pushed herself to her feet and walked off. She didn't stop when she got to the edge of the field. She kept right on walking, I assumed heading back to her car in the school lot.

It was then that I knew for sure that her dreams hadn't been dreams at all. She'd seen Summer eating a pig like a wild animal and she'd seen Trinity. Trinity was back.

CHAPTER TEN

After I'd made myself another sandwich for dinner, I lurked around the living room for a while, a bit uncomfortable with my room after having been attacked inside it not once, but twice. I could only avoid it for so long, however, when Mom came stumbling in at the inordinately-early hour of 8:30, forcing me into hiding for the rest of the night. Fortunately, she went straight to her room and didn't come back out, a fact for which I was incredibly grateful. I didn't need a repeat of the previous night; I was still licking my wounds from that run-in.

I spent the next hour or so watching my window uncomfortably, hoping for Bo, but dreading anyone else. I still didn't know what had become of Drew and now with Trinity and Summer on the loose, I felt like I had to look over my shoulder at every turn.

I kept waiting for Bo to appear, hoping I'd see him. I felt like the buzz in my blood was fading and I didn't like it. It was comforting to me, feeling that intense tie to him, and I wanted it back, strong and sure.

Feeling more deflated and paranoid as time went by, I decided I'd call Savannah and confirm tomorrow night's dinner, maybe chat with her for a while. She would no doubt provide a much-needed distraction, as well as some amusement, something I had far too little of in my life of late. Besides, I needed to see if she'd heard from Devon, or seen him or imagined him, whatever was happening there.

I dug through my bag for my phone, but couldn't find it. There was a time when that thing was practically glued to my palm. Back in the days of Trinity and Drew, my phone rang constantly. But now, not so much. That wasn't necessarily a bad thing, just different. I had to admit that, at times, I felt very disconnected and lonely. It wouldn't be nearly so bad if Bo wasn't supposedly missing while he spent most of his time trying to track down the people responsible for screwing up his life. If that wasn't the case, I could see him more often, and in the daylight, too.

With a sigh, I grabbed my keys and headed for my car. My phone must've dropped out in there and it looked like I was definitely going to need a diversion.

Padding down the walk barefoot, I unlocked my car door and leaned in to see if I could find my phone. When I couldn't locate it, I went back inside for the house phone. I dialed my own number and listened to it ring. I walked back to my bedroom and stood just inside the door. I listened closely for the music to Jaws, which is what my ring tone was set for when Mom or Dad called. No Jaws ringing in there, so I went back outside and put my head inside the car again. No Jaws ringing in there either.

Frustrated and mystified, I wracked my brain for what might've become of my phone. And then I remembered that

Carly had asked to borrow it to call her boyfriend and tell him to pick her up at school for their date, rather than meeting her at the theater. Her phone's battery was dead. I'd handed it to her and, when she'd finished, she told me she'd laid it on top of my bag. But now, I couldn't remember grabbing it as I left. I'd no doubt picked up my duffel and headed for the car, probably knocking my phone off into the grass in front of the bleachers.

"Crap," I said to the stale air inside my car. I couldn't very well leave it outside all night. If someone hadn't already stepped on it, it would be ruined by morning; it was supposed to rain tonight. And if it got ruined, my parents would kill me. It had taken me a month to convince them that I needed an iPhone.

Looking around me at the deep shadows, I was torn. I really needed to go get that phone, but I hated to go alone after dark. It's not like I'd had a shortage of reasons to be afraid of the dark. But then again, if recent events were any indication, I'd be more likely to be attacked if I stayed at home in my room than if I took a quick trip back to the school.

Thoughts of my parents skinning me alive over that stupid iPhone won out and I slid behind the wheel, bare feet and all, and started the engine. I'd be back in a flash and Mom wouldn't even know I was gone.

Zipping down the side roads and back streets, I was racing through the school parking lot in no time. As my headlights stretched out in front of me, they illuminated a small gray hatchback that I knew to be Carly's. It appeared that she and her boyfriend weren't back from the movies yet.

Ignoring the yellow lines and No Parking signage that skirted the building, I pulled right up against the back of the field house, shining my lights directly at the bleachers, and pushed the gear shift into park. Taking a deep breath, I took a second to scan the darkness before hopping out and dashing to the stands.

I went to the very end of the first row of bleachers, which is where I always sat my stuff. I walked gingerly in a tight circle, brushing my foot through the grass blades as I searched for the little black rectangle. When I didn't find it, I retraced the route I'd taken when I left. About ten or fifteen feet from the bleachers, my toes scraped against something hard in the grass and I stopped to look. Sure enough, it was my phone.

I picked it up and high tailed it back to my car, imagining all sorts of creepy things lurking in the shadows, gnashing their teeth at me. Hopping quickly into the driver's seat, I locked the door behind me. I felt the urge to squeal, all my senses on alert, my muscles jumping with anxiety. When it appeared that nothing was stalking me, however, I calmed and shifted into drive, steering the car back the way I'd come.

When my headlights hit Carly's hatchback this time, it was from the front, the lights shining through her windshield. I saw Carly's head behind the steering wheel. I wondered if she'd fought with Ethan. The way her head was bent, with her chin on her chest, it looked like she was crying.

I pulled up beside her and put my car in park again, getting out and walking around to the driver's side. I leaned down and pecked on the foggy window, but Carly didn't raise her head.

"Carly," I said. "Roll down the window."

Still she didn't lift her head. I raised my hand to wipe away the moisture from the glass, but it was on the inside.

As a last resort, I reached for the handle and pulled the door open.

"Carly, what—"

The words died in my throat when Carly's body slithered lifelessly from the driver's seat and rolled out into the parking lot.

The light from my headlights shone under the car, shining on half of her body. Everything I could see was covered in blood. Carly's throat was laying open and the front of her shirt was missing, torn away to reveal that her mid-section had been eaten away, leaving nothing but a gaping hole surrounded by jagged bits of flesh and entrails.

Saliva poured into my mouth as everything in my body rebelled against what I was seeing. Numbly, I took several steps backward until I could move no further, forced to my knees where my sandwich and everything else that was still in my stomach found its way onto the pavement.

I squeezed my eyes shut, no longer able to tolerate the sight of my friend lying there, mutilated, in the school parking lot. I knew I should get up, but my legs refused to work.

Tears streamed down my face as my body continued to heave. When there was nothing left in my belly and my ribs ached from exertion, I pushed myself to my feet.

With stiff fingers, I took my phone from my pocket and dialed 911. When the operator answered, I reported where I was and what I had witnessed. The bland woman's voice assured me that a unit had been dispatched and was on their way to me.

I stood, dumbstruck, staring at Carly's wide-open eyes and tear-stained face, unable to look any lower, unwilling to take in even one more detail of the horrific death she'd suffered.

When I heard sirens in the distance, I forced my rubbery legs into motion and I turned to walk around the hood of Carly's car and make my way to my own. When I'd opened my door and flopped down into the driver's seat, I looked out into the darkness, the cold fingers of shock working their way into my chest.

That's when I saw her.

Standing at the edge of the row of pine trees that lined the school's drive was Summer. Though she looked nothing like the Summer that I knew, she still looked familiar enough for me to recognize who it was.

Her long brown hair hung in thick matted tangles on either side of her pale face. Her complexion had a sallow look to it, easily detectable despite the blood that ringed her mouth. Her hollow eyes were yellowed and rimmed in darkness. It was from them that she watched me.

Her white hoodie was filthy, covered in blood and dirt, and her chest heaved beneath it. One sleeve was torn off, revealing the pale, dirty skin of her arm as it hung limply at her side. Her fingers worked in a grasping motion, almost thoughtlessly, like she wasn't even aware she was doing it. She just continued to stare, watching me blankly, as my heart slammed against my sternum.

I was afraid to move. She seemed to be looking through me more than at me, as if she didn't really know I was there. I didn't want to risk changing that. My fear was overwhelming, but it hadn't yet drowned out rational thought. True panic didn't set in until I saw one corner of her bloody mouth tilt up in a vicious sneer. It was then that I realized that not only did she see me, but she recognized me. And her smile said I'd be seeing her again.

The sirens were drawing closer and, just then, the first cop car came skidding into the parking lot, blue lights flashing from the roof. I'd shifted my gaze from Summer for a fraction of a second to see the police arrive, and when I looked back, she was gone. Only the residual wave of some pine branches assured me that I hadn't altogether imagined her being there.

Of course, once the official circus began, I was grilled relentlessly. I told several different law enforcement and medical examiner people everything that had happened, all but the part about seeing Summer. That was something, for better or worse, that I'd decided I'd best keep to myself.

For one thing, they might think I'm crazy, which wouldn't do me any favors. But also, I thought it might save more lives if Bo dealt with her. If she was as hard to kill as Lucius insinuated that she might be, a lot of people could get hurt trying to stop her if they started looking for her.

It was almost two hours later when I was finally allowed to get back into my car. The crime scene people had looked it over with a fine-toothed comb, searching for any evidence that I might've lied about my story. I could only assume that when they let me get in it, they'd decided I wasn't the bad guy here.

As I was starting the car, one officer had the nerve to saunter up to my window and chastise me for driving without shoes. I gawked at him, mouth agape, as I fought the urge to flip him the bird and peel out of the parking lot. It's not like I'd had a bad enough day already or anything.

Let's throw caution and compassion to the wind and make it a pile-on-Ridley kind of day, I thought bitterly as I glared at his reflection in my rearview mirror as I drove away. Barefoot.

By the time I got home, I was jittery and shaken. The entire ordeal had been horrific beyond anything I could imagine. And considering what all I'd seen in the past months, that was saying a lot.

I shut off the engine, staring sullenly at the dark house. My mother was probably passed out, oblivious to the fact that I had even been out. She would have no idea that I sat in the driveway, afraid—deeply, profoundly afraid—or that I'd seen the interior of a friend's abdomen. She would have no idea that lately I had been feeling like my entire world was crumbling, spinning out of my control, happiness and normalcy far out of reach.

No, she would have no idea that any of those things were going on in her remaining daughter's life. But the worst part was that, even if she did, she likely wouldn't care, any if at all. Her heart was in the Westbrook Cemetery, buried beneath six feet of earth with the decaying body of my sister. She had nothing left for those of us who lived, nothing but a few hours of pretense every weekend.

My growl bounced off the ceiling of my quiet car. "Stop feeling sorry for yourself, Ridley," I ground between my gritted teeth.

Wrenching the car door open, I got out and slammed it behind me. I was all but stomping up the sidewalk, angrily preoccupied, when I heard the shuffling noise in the yard to my left.

I stopped mid-stride, my pulse beating heavily inside the lump of terror that had lodged in my esophagus. I was almost afraid to look, to see who or what was coming for me this time. But on some level, I knew I didn't really have to look to know who it was. On some level, I knew. It was Summer.

When I looked in the direction of the noise, she was ambling across the yard toward me. She wasn't moving very quickly or even in a manner that was distinctly threatening, but it scared the crap out of me nonetheless.

With a yip, I somehow managed to contain my full-fledged, five-alarm, wake-the-dead scream as I bolted for the door. My frantic hands fumbled for the key that opened the front door, the one I'd been considerate enough to lock behind me when I left. Despite my mother's drastic changes since Izzy's death, I still didn't want any boogers walking right into the house and eating her.

When I found it, I tried to steady my trembling fingers and slide the key into the lock. I glanced back over my shoulder; it was the only mistake that I had time for.

Summer's almost casual lumbering disappeared as she crouched down and flew across the grass toward me. She was upon me before I could fill my lungs with enough air to let out the scream I'd been holding inside.

She moved incredibly quickly. Not vampire quick, but much faster than I imagined most humans could. And when she reached me, I knew instantly that her strength was enhanced as well. When her claw-like fingers wrapped round my upper arms, it felt like giant talons sinking into my flesh. I actually felt the density of my bones giving way. I wondered if I didn't have Bo's blood still giving me a little extra oomph if she would've broken my arms.

In a motion so fast it made my head spin, she threw me to the ground and jumped on top of me. The rest was a blur. It seemed that she had ten mouths and dozens of hands and they were all biting and pinching and ripping and tearing, all at once. I felt pain from my navel upward.

I thrashed and batted my arms, kicked my legs and bucked my hips, but she was impossible to dislodge. Nothing I did seemed to have any effect on her. I couldn't fend her off and I couldn't slow her down.

I heard an eerie, hair-raising giggle and I knew that she was actually enjoying herself, playing with her food before she got down to the business of eating. And that put the fear of God into me. What would happen when she stopped playing?

Sucking in as much air as my compressed lungs would hold, I opened my mouth and let out a blood-curdling scream. Rather than scare her off, however, it seemed only to incite Summer. Her movements became more pointed, more frantic and vicious, like she knew her time was limited, that help might be on the way.

But then she stilled, stopping to look down at me. Her mad eyes met mine for one breath, one long heartbeat, during which I knew that she was aware, she was malicious, and she was determined. She was going to kill me, but not before she tasted my flesh, ate her fill like she did with Carly. She wanted me to feel fear, to feel pain, to feel her teeth.

And then she was gone.

When her weight was suddenly no longer holding me down, I lay on the ground, confused, for several seconds before my freedom sank into my addled, terrified brain. When it did, I scrambled to my feet and ran straight for the door. I didn't care why or how it happened; I just cared that I had a brief reprieve and I had no intention of wasting it.

I had just unlocked the door and was about to step inside when I heard a crack that sounded like thunder, one that shook the front step. Against my better judgment, I looked behind me.

I saw Summer pick herself up off the ground where she'd landed in a heap at the bottom of a splintered thirty-foot-tall oak tree. Quickly springing back onto her feet, Summer stood. I thought she was turning back toward me, but she kept swiveling until she was facing a huge bush that loomed just to the left of the front porch.

"Just who I wanted to see. What did you think of my handiwork?" Summer asked in a child-like sing-song voice.

"She was my grandmother," a low feminine voice said from behind the bush. I knew that voice.

"And she was delicious."

"How could you do that to an old woman?"

"How could you do this to me?"

For several tense seconds, an uncomfortable silence stretched across the yard. But then I caught movement from the bush.

"I'm not finished yet," Trinity said, stepping from behind the bush.

"Give it your best shot," Summer said, her lips twisting into a cold sneer.

With an animal-like scream, Trinity bolted across the grass. To my eye, she was nothing more than a pale streak that smelled strongly of dank earth.

When she hit Summer, the thud of flesh meeting flesh reverberated through the air. Trinity wrapped her small body around Summer's and went straight for her throat. It looked as if Trinity's teeth were buried deep in Summer's neck when Summer brought her hands up to Trinity's mouth and dug her fingers in, yanking Trinity's lower jaw with one bone-crushing jerk. Trinity cried out, letting go of Summer and stepping away. I could see that her jaw was broken. It hung limply from her upper teeth, jutting sharply off to one side.

Bringing her palm to her chin, Trinity tried to push her mandible back into place, but Summer wasn't finished. Launching herself at Trinity, Summer knocked her to the ground and pinned her arms to her sides. I could see that

Trinity was struggling to free herself, but she could barely move, not much more effective than I'd been against Summer.

Summer's chilly laughter floated out around her as she taunted Trinity.

"What? Aren't you strong enough to take care of little ol' me? You didn't seem to have any trouble when you bit me the first time, now did you?"

Trinity wrestled, to no avail. She grunted and groaned, but she never said a word, unable to speak with her jaw in the shape it was.

"What's the matter, Trinity? Cat got your tongue?"

And with that, Summer leaned down and took Trinity's displaced tongue into her mouth and bit down. Trinity made a squealing noise in the back of her throat, but I saw no more. I had to turn my head away, though I couldn't bring myself to move into the house.

I heard a muffled crackling sound and more moans from Trinity. The hairs on my arms rose and prickled. Another crackling sound and more moans had me wracking my brain for what I could do to help, but I knew I was no match for Summer. Besides, I wasn't entirely sure that Trinity was someone I was willing to risk my life for.

Some rustling sounds were followed by a shriek, only this time it sounded like Summer's. I had to look, if only for a second.

I saw Summer shoot across the grass like a rocket. At first I wasn't sure how Trinity had managed to get her off of her, much less send her all the way across the yard. But then I saw who Summer was aiming at. It was Bo.

When she hit him, it slowed her down, but she still managed to get him to the ground. I never would've imagined that Summer could possess a strength like that, but I saw firsthand how easily she dispatched Trinity and she was a vampire. And I knew how strong vampires were.

Bo wrestled with her for a few seconds before pushing her off, sending her soaring through the air. I was relieved that he was able to fight her off, but it barely phased Summer. She leapt immediately to her feet and went back after Bo. He darted this way and that, but she was perfectly able to keep up with him, catching up to him and wrapping her thin arms around his torso. With one vicious bite, Summer sank her teeth into the side of his face where his jaw hinged. Though her teeth appeared to be smooth and blunt, it was apparent that they were sharp and deadly.

Bo made a noise I'd never heard before and brought his arms up between their bodies, where he pushed out, fast and hard. Summer lost her hold on him just enough for Bo to free his hands and grab her right arm.

In one quick move, Bo ducked and at the same time yanked on Summer's arm as he moved around behind her. Rather than a snap like breaking bone, I heard a dull *thunk* sound, like concrete busting or rock being split. Her bones sounded petrified.

With a maniacal laugh, Summer swung around and leveled a punch right at Bo's head, staggering him to the side. When he let her arm go, it hung at her side, twisted behind her back at an odd angle.

Wrapping the fingers of her good hand around the wrist of her wounded arm, Summer jerked until, with a nauseating pop and squish, her arm was back in a semi-normal position. And then she attacked again.

She scrambled toward him as if she had a thousand arms and a thousand legs, all battering and grabbing at once. She maneuvered him back against the tree she'd split only minutes before.

Summer ripped and tore at Bo, clawed and snatched at him, nipped and bit at him. Across the lawn, I could hear her teeth clicking together as she snapped them at his face. Bo was so quick he managed to avoid them for the most part, but he was struggling to contain her.

I gasped when Bo lost his control on her and her teeth found purchase in the flesh of his forearm. She shook her head from side to side until she came away with a mouthful of bloody flesh. I could see the golf-ball sized chunk missing from Bo's arm.

Bo reached behind his head and snapped off a large branch as easily as if it were a twig. As Summer was coming back for more, Bo brought the makeshift stake around and buried it in Summer's chest. And it stopped her. For a moment.

Looking down at the branch and then back up at Bo, I could tell that Summer was confused, but that only lasted for a few seconds. Summer quickly recovered, and when she did, she giggled. It was an eerie, dainty, crazy-little-girl giggle that sent an uneasy tingle slithering down my spine.

But then, Summer did the unthinkable. In one smooth motion, so fast it was almost a blur, she pulled the stake out of her own chest and shoved it deep into Bo's.

I was stunned. Shocked. It was as if the whole thing happened in slow motion.

"No!" I yelled.

For an instant the world stopped spinning and time stood still. I couldn't see the exact placement of the strike and I wasn't yet completely convinced that Bo was the boy who can't be killed. So for that moment, I was terrified beyond description. I waited breathlessly to see if Bo would move. I willed him to be alright, willed him to fight back.

My mind struggled to grasp how Summer—just a skinny teenaged girl—could actually hurt Bo. It was hard to believe, but it was the nature of what Summer had become. Lucius had been right; it seemed that she was nearly invincible.

My legs finally came alive and I sprang into motion. They carried me quickly across the grass. I'd hesitated to put my life on the line for Trinity, but there was nothing on earth that could keep me from risking it all for Bo.

As I drew closer to them, I saw Bo reach between them and pull out the stake. I let out the breath I'd been holding. I was so relieved my legs felt like jelly. Afraid that they could no longer support me, I slowed to a stop a few feet from where the two fought.

Bo and Summer were so focused on one another that I never would have expected for Summer to turn toward me, to even remember that I was there. But she did, and because I'd been nearly crippled with relief, I was slow to move.

She landed on me, taking me to the ground effortlessly. I was on my back again and this time, she wasn't toying with her food. She went right for my neck with her bloody mouth.

When her face was so close it blurred in my vision, I closed my eyes. I knew my fate and there was nothing I could do to stop it. If Bo couldn't defeat her, then I didn't stand a chance.

I felt more pressure on my chest, like someone was pushing down on me, more than just Summer's weight, and then I felt a warm splatter spray my face and run down the sides of my neck. I had no idea what it was, but I wasn't going to open my eyes to find out. There were some things that a person was just better off not seeing. Brutal, disgusting death coming right at you was one of them.

I thought it was strange when I felt Summer's body slump down onto mine. It was as if her arms had given out, and she just collapsed onto me.

She lay atop me, warm and motionless. When several seconds had passed and she had yet to rip out my jugular or bite off my face, I cracked one eyelid. What I saw took my rattled brain a few seconds to process.

I saw Bo. He stood above me, looking down at his hands. Between them, he was holding Summer's head.

CHAPTER ELEVEN

Bo was amazing that night as I gave in to the urge to let hysteria have its way. It had been a long time coming and when I finally succumbed, I fell to pieces.

From the moment it set in that he was holding my friend's head in his hands up until I fell asleep in his arms hours later, Bo was wonderfully tender and kind.

He'd very gently laid Summer's head down somewhere out of my line of sight and then picked me up and carried me inside. He didn't stop until I was bawling my eyes out in the warm cocoon of my bathroom, buried chin deep in hot, frothy bubbles.

Sometime later, when my fingers were well and truly pruned, Bo had come back for me. He'd helped me out and discreetly assisted me to dry off and dress. Then he had carried me to my bed and laid me down, turning me on my side and spooning me from behind. He had lovingly stroked my hair and my arm, sweetly kissed my shoulder and my neck and softly whispered beautiful things into my ear until I fell asleep.

My last memory, after I had finally calmed enough to consider sleep, was of Bo tracing my cheekbone with the tip of his finger and his cool breath tickling my jaw.

"I'm so sorry, Ridley. I'm so, so sorry," he murmured.

The next morning, my first thought when I opened my eyes, the one right after Bo of course, was of Trinity. I sat up and searched the room for some sign of Bo or his glimmer, but it appeared that he was already gone.

With haste and an urgency I hadn't felt before, I threw back the covers and got ready for school. On the way, I dialed Aisha's number over and over and over again, but got no answer. I prayed that I wasn't too late.

I'd made up my mind that it was finally time to tell those that I cared about, those that were close to me and appeared to be in danger, that the ghost stories were real—and that they have very sharp teeth.

Every mouth at school, of course, was talking about what had happened with Carly. I was inundated with questions. I suppose it was just human nature, but it was very disturbing to see, up close and personal, how much people relished the details of an atrocity like that. Everyone wanted to know what exactly had happened to her, right down to what she was wearing and what her insides looked like.

Needless to say, I had very little to say to anybody. Not only did I not have any desire to disrespect Carly by sharing details like that, the police had specifically asked me not to tell anyone the specifics of the crime scene until they gave me direct permission to do so. They even gave me a little incentive to do as they asked. It came in the form of a veiled threat where they would charge me with obstruction of justice if I made the mistake of revealing something important to any of my friends.

I wanted to tell the police that most of my friends were either dead or monsters, but I didn't. I just nodded and agreed in all the right places.

I couldn't find Aisha all morning. Between classes I called her phone, but I always got her voice mail. With every hour that ticked by, I held onto the hope that she'd be at school by lunchtime, like she had on Monday. Unfortunately, lunch came and went with still no sign of Aisha.

Since there was no cheerleading practice tonight, I decided to drive by Aisha's house before going home. I wasn't really surprised to see that there were no cars in the driveway and no indication that anyone was home. Both her parents worked, so...

After knocking on every door I could get to, I hopped back in my car, frustrated. I promised myself that I'd try again after dinner at Savannah's. Surely someone would be home by then.

It was during the drive to Savannah's house, as I was reliving events from the previous night, that I put two and two together from the short conversation between Summer and Trinity. I finally remembered why the name of the elderly attack victim in Sumter sounded familiar. Maggie Jenner was Trinity's grandmother. She made organic soaps and shampoos and sold them in a small store in downtown Sumter. Trinity had given me a set of lavender bath products two years ago for Christmas when she'd drawn my name in the Secret Santa. Obviously, ours were never that secret.

Trinity's reaction over the death of her grandmother puzzled me. As cold and heartless as she was when she was human, I had no doubts, especially after the accident and what she did to Savannah, that she was even less conscionable as a vampire.

But then there was her reaction to her grandmother's grisly death. She hadn't sounded heartless; she'd sounded a bit heartbroken actually. Was it possible that Trinity might still have a decent streak, somewhere deep down?

She'd been obsessed with Devon and had probably absconded with him the night of the accident. That's what Bo and I had both concluded. Yet, Savannah said that Devon was back, that she'd seen him and talked to him. Was it possible that Trinity hadn't killed him? That she'd merely captured him and then had a change of heart and let him go?

By the time I pulled up at the curb in front of Savannah's house, I had decided that I'd tell Savannah about Trinity and Lars. If Devon was really back and I was wrong about Trinity, then Savannah could be in danger. The very least I could do was to tell her the truth and warn her.

I figured that Savannah would be in her room, as she'd been every other time I'd visited her, and I planned to tell her right away. Unwittingly, however, Savannah threw a kink in my plan. When Mr. Grant let me in, Savannah was in the kitchen helping him cook.

"Get in here and help me cut vegetables. It's your fault I've been put to work and only the meanest type of person would give a knife to a blind kid," Savannah called from the kitchen.

I blushed and Mr. Grant patted my arm, closing the front door behind me.

"She's kidding. She just takes some getting used to."

I just smiled politely and followed him into the kitchen.

Savannah was at the island, carefully cutting carrots and dumping them into a salad bowl. Watching her wield the sharp instrument did bring Mr. Grant's judgment into question.

"What she doesn't tell you is that she blackmailed me into letting her use the knife."

Oh. Now that sounded like Savannah. Again, I smiled.

"What can I do to help?"

"You can wash your hands and cut some peppers," Savannah said without hesitation.

"I can do that."

After I cleaned up, I joined Savannah at the island and helped her dice vegetables and prepare the salad and toppings for dinner. It was the most fun I'd ever had helping out in the kitchen. The banter between Savannah and her father was light and playful, overflowing with love and affection. Even more than before, I envied their relationship.

"Gourmet- ha! I could make a better lasagna than you any day of the week."

"In your dreams, little girl," he said and then turned to me. "Heather was a terrible cook and Vanna's just like her."

My heart stopped. "Heather?"

Mr. Grant smiled. "Yes. Savannah's mother. She was a terrible cook, too."

"Was?"

"I told you that my mother died, Ridley, remember?"

"That's right you did. You said she drowned, right?"

Both Savannah and her father nodded, suddenly very quiet.

Surely that had to be a coincidence. I mean, there was just no way. Was there?

"I'm sorry. Maybe we should change the subject." I couldn't think of anything else to say.

Though the subject was changed, the tone for the rest of the evening was noticeably more somber. I could've kicked myself for asking about Savannah's mom. I felt even worse for thinking such a ridiculous and terrible thing about her, for thinking she could be the Heather. But still, I was very anxious to talk to Bo, tell him about Savannah's mother and see what he thought.

By the time dinner was over and I'd helped clean up, I thought to start making my excuses to leave. Turns out I didn't have to.

From my pocket, my cell phone chirped. When I answered it, I was greeted by the silky smooth baritone of Sebastian Aiello.

"Ridley, this is Sebastian."

"Yes, sir. How are you?"

"I'm fine. I got your number from your mother. I hope you don't mind."

"Of course not. What's up?"

"Well, right now I'm in desperate need of your services. I know it's last minute and I'm sorry to bother you, but is there any way that you could watch Lilly for me? Nothing too long. Say, two hours? I'd even double your pay," he added slyly.

I chewed my lip as I thought. I really wanted to go to Aisha's again and then talk to Bo. But, I could continue to call Aisha from Sebastian's and Bo wasn't likely to show up until later, so what was the harm in spending some time with Lilly and making almost a hundred bucks in the meantime?

"I can do that. What time do you need me?"

"Could you be here in the next thirty minutes?"

"Sure. I'll see you soon."

"Great! Thanks, Ridley."

When I got off the phone, my end of the conversation had already made my excuses to Savannah and her dad for me.

"Go. We've got the rest," Savannah said, spreading plastic wrap over the top of a bowl.

"Are you sure? I hate to eat and run."

"Sure, sure," Savannah said with a mischievous smile.

"Really, I never—"

"Kidding, Ridley. Go on. All we have left to do is put the leftovers in the fridge."

"Are you sure?"

"I'm positive."

I looked to Mr. Grant.

"She's right. We've got it under control. Besides, you've already helped with the hard part. Guests aren't supposed to do dishes," he explained, frowning.

"It's the least I could do since you were kind enough to have me."

"It was our pleasure, wasn't it, Vanna?"

"I suppose," she sighed, rolling her eyes dramatically, but then she looked at me and winked. "Seriously, go on. We're good. I'm just glad you came."

And when I looked at Savannah's expression, I could see that she really meant that. She looked happy and relaxed and more carefree than I'd seen her in a while.

On my way to Sebastian's, I called Mom's cell phone. When she answered, I could hear the typical bar sounds in the background—glasses clinking, people laughing, Mom slurring.

Briefly, I explained where I was going and, as I suspected, she agreed wholeheartedly, not for one second remembering her supposed concern over me being out after dark by myself. Dad wasn't around. She didn't have to pretend anymore.

Chagrined, I hung up and tried to put her out of my mind. Savannah and her dad, too. It wasn't helping matters with my own family by comparing them to a normal relationship, so I pushed all families out of my head except the one I was going to help right now.

When I rang the bell, Sebastian answered the door in a black turtle neck sweater and black pants. I was once again impressed with his incredible handsomeness.

"Thank you so much, Ridley. I promise I won't be gone long," he preempted me, holding the door open so I could enter.

"No problem."

"This should be easy money for you. Lilly had a doctor's appointment today. Had to get her next round of vaccinations. It wore her out. She's already asleep, so you don't need to do anything more than listen for her in case she wakes up."

"Oh, ok," I said, a little disappointed. Not only was I looking forward to the distraction, but I liked Lilly and I hated that I wouldn't really get to see her.

"The housekeeper had to make an unexpected trip out of town. That's why the last minute call. Sorry about that."

"No problem," I repeated.

"I just made a strawberry colada smoothie. Virgin, of course. Help yourself. It's in the fridge," Sebastian explained, walking toward the kitchen.

"Thanks."

"Alright, make yourself at home. I'll be back in a couple hours."

With a polite smile, Sebastian grabbed his keys off the counter by the kitchen door, waved casually and disappeared into the garage.

I stood in the kitchen for a few minutes before I plopped down on a barstool with a humph. This was going to be worse than being at home.

Flopping my purse up on the bar, I walked to the fridge and pulled out the pitcher of strawberry colada that Sebastian made. It looked like Pepto Bismol. I wiggled the lid back and sniffed.

"Mmm, coconut," I said to the empty kitchen. I love coconut!

After snooping enough to locate the glasses, which were conveniently located right next to the refrigerator, I poured myself some of the thick treat and meandered into the den.

I eyed the entertainment center, thinking of picking out a movie, but I wasn't really in the mood, so I walked down the hall to peep in on Lilly. She was sleeping soundly, her little hand tucked under her cheek like the angel that she was. The sight tugged on my heartstrings. Swallowing the *aww* that lurked in my throat, I backed out and closed the door snugly behind me.

With a bored and frustrated sigh, I turned and made my way back down the hall, stopping as I passed Sebastian's study. It was dark in there, unlike the last time, when I'd been lured inside by the showcased and spotlighted book about vampires. Just the thought of the book and all the wonders (and possibly answers) that it held made my feet itch to go inside. But I resisted.

Moving on through the house, I opened doors and looked into all sorts of rooms that I probably had no business looking in. It was as I was passing through to the den again that I heard the noise.

It sounded like someone dropping something onto the floor in one of the rooms above me. Only there wasn't supposed to be anyone here besides me and Lilly.

A little niggle of trepidation worked its way down my back and legs, bringing every fine hair follicle on my body to attention. Setting my untouched drink down, I backtracked until I came to the steps that led to the second story.

The gently turning sweep of the dark wood staircase looked fairly benign, as did the beautiful red and gold runner that streaked up the middle of the tread. I reached out and laid my hand on the rich, elegantly curved banister. It was cool beneath my palm.

With one foot on the first step, I hesitated. I'd never been to the second story. I'd never bothered exploring it and Lilly had never even so much as mentioned it. Her room, as well as Sebastian's, was on the first floor, so I hadn't really had a reason to go up there. Until now.

My fingers twitched. I wished they were gripping my cell phone. Not that it would matter. Bo hadn't had a cell phone since his supposed disappearance. His mother (who apparently was not his mother at all) had dropped his plan. And it wouldn't do me any good to call the police. The things I was afraid of were not things the police could help me with.

I had just about talked myself out of going upstairs when I heard the noise again. I looked around nervously. It was when my eyes lit on Lilly's door that I realized that I owed it to her, to her safety, to check it out.

Keeping my tread as light as possible, I mounted the steps to the next story. The air smelled stale and musty, as if the entire floor was rarely ever used. It being only Sebastian and Lilly, I didn't doubt that at all.

From where I landed, the hall split left and right with only one door straight ahead. I stopped and held my breath to listen before venturing in either direction.

When I heard nothing, I walked slowly forward and twisted the knob for the first door. Inside it was a room full of furniture, every piece covered in a protective plastic drape. The hardwoods were dull, lying beneath a generous layer of dust that was very obviously undisturbed. Quietly, I shut the door and turned to proceed down the hall.

I chose the left side of the second level first, as it would contain the rooms that were directly over the kitchen and den, which is where I was when I'd first heard the noise.

I followed the runner until I came to the first of three doors. I leaned in, pressing my ear lightly to the door, listening for sounds. But it was quiet, so I turned the knob and eased the wood panel open. Inside, I found much the same thing as I had in the other room.

Closing it, I made my way to door number two, which proved to be another repeat, a large room full of plastic-covered furniture and a ton of dust. It was behind door number three that I noticed a change.

The hinges creaked as I opened the third door. I poked my head in and saw the familiar lumps of covered furniture. The departure from the scenes in the other two rooms occurred on the floor. The thick layer of dust that covered the hardwoods had been disturbed in this room. By the looks of the clean prints, I guessed that the tracks had been laid fairly recently.

The footprints appeared to be in the shape of a man's dress shoe, and the foot was not at all small. For a second, I wondered if maybe Sebastian had been in the room recently. That would account for the disturbance in the dust as well as the type of print it looked to be.

That thought made me feel a bit better for all of about ten seconds, as long as it took my eyes to track the footprints to where they disappeared against the wall on the other side of the room. It wasn't until then that I noticed that there were no returning footsteps; only those going toward the wall, away from the door.

My heart rate picked up as I mulled over the wisdom of crossing the room to follow the prints. Part of my brain remained calm, reminding me that there was likely a rational explanation for what I was seeing. But then there was the other half of my brain, the portion that had seen horrible things, witnessed horrible things, knew of too many horrible things—it suggested that I turn tail and run. Fast.

Steeling myself against the fear and unease that was quickly surfacing inside me, I opened the door wider and stepped inside. I stopped and listened. Still, there was silence. I wondered for a second if I could've imagined hearing something. But deep down, I knew. I knew I'd heard something.

I tiptoed across the room, careful to step exactly where the person before me had stepped. I had to stretch to get from print to print, which further supported my theory that the tracks belonged to a man, probably Sebastian's. The stride was long, a lot longer than mine.

When I'd reached the other side of the room, I could see a faint scrape mark where something had brushed the dust away in an arch, similar to that of a door opening. And yet there was no door, only a blank wall.

The footprints clearly disappeared into that wall, so I began feeling around, rubbing my hands across the floral wallpaper, hoping to find...something. Considering the age and type of house this was, a hidden passageway wouldn't really surprise me.

I jumped when I heard another noise. My heart filled with dread when I realized that it had, in fact, come from the other side of the wall, the one I was standing in front of. I also noticed that the noise had caused a puff of dust to leak out around a crack in the wallpaper.

I ran my fingertip along the seam. At about waist level, my finger slipped into a dip. I bent down to look at it and realized that the paper was peeled away right in the center of a flower, making the dark crescent underneath nearly invisible. Hooking my finger into the indentation, I pulled.

And a door popped open.

It only opened a tiny crack, but my pulse started fluttering wildly in my chest. I listened for any sounds of movement, like someone might have heard me and turned to come after me. But there was absolute, eerie stillness. All I could hear was the shallow pant of my breathing against the backdrop of my pulse pounding away in my ears.

Carefully, I pulled the door until it was open wide enough for me to slide inside. I left it ajar in case I had to make a hasty escape, which gave me cold chills just to think about.

The first thing I noticed was that I smelled roses. For some reason, that gave me pause, but I couldn't figure out why. The only smell I associated with roses was Lucius's luxurious basement.

When my eyes had adjusted to the dim light, I saw the orangey glow of candle light sparkling like a thousand tiny diamonds in the spider web that hung thickly in the little hallway. It was evident that a path had been cut recently, as if someone had walked right through the middle of them.

Silently, I tiptoed toward the light, toward the mouth of the short corridor where a room opened up at the end. When I got to the point where if I continued on, I would no longer be in the shadows, I stopped walking and leaned slowly around the corner to peer into the room.

What I saw both confused and concerned me. It was Lilly. She was lying atop a cot that sat in the center of a circle of dozens of white pillar candles. She was still fast asleep, lying on her side with her pink lips parted ever so slightly. My heart squeezed at the sight of her. I didn't know what it was, but something about Lilly touched me — deeply.

But why was she up here? In a hidden room, surrounded by candles?

The questions had no sooner entered my mind when I heard a woman's voice break the silence.

"Mmm, that smell. I can almost taste your sweet blood, warm and sticky, flowing over my tongue like silk."

I stilled instantly. I wasn't even breathing. I thought at first the woman was talking to someone else, but then, with a lightning bolt of panic that shot straight to my toes, I realized that I recognized the voice. And she was talking to me.

Just as I was turning to run, I felt a breeze stir my hair. And when I looked up, I was face to face with a beautiful red head that I'd seen before. My head swam dizzily, my mind rebelling against what I concluded.

No! It can't be! It just can't be, I was thinking, but all the while, that other part of me, the rational calm part, was telling me that it was very much true.

"Heather," I whispered, stunned beyond description.

"Bravo," she said, moving around to my back.

I was in shock. Savannah's mother was standing right behind me. I recognized her from the photos in Savannah's room. And her name was Heather; Mr. Grant had mentioned it. She was the same Heather that Bo had been searching for, the one and only. Though I had no proof, I was certain of it. I knew it, knew it without a doubt, knew it in my bones. It was her. And she'd found me. Again.

It jarred me when I finally placed that vaguely familiar floral scent. I'd smelled it, the scent of roses, in my bedroom when I'd been attacked and bitten, as well as at Denise's house when I'd gone to visit her and caught someone there. It had been this woman—Heather.

Savannah had been right. Her mother had visited her. What Savannah didn't know was that her mother is alive. Sort of. She's a vampire. Somehow, though she was unable to see anything else, Savannah could see vampires.

And then I remembered yet another alarming thought. She could see Devon, too.

My racing mind stopped its erratic flitting when I felt the hair at my neck move. Soft, warm fingers brushed it away and my focus was once again sharply concentrated on the person at my back.

I knew I needed to flee, to get out of there, away from her, but I couldn't just leave. I wasn't the only one at risk. As terrified as I was for myself, for what she might do to me, I had to consider Lilly. If possible, I was even more horrified at what the woman might do to her. She was just a child.

Before I could follow my fears to any kind of conclusion or come up with some sort of plan to get us out of there alive, I heard the quiet words that I'd heard once before. And I knew what was coming.

"Shh," she breathed. Then, in the husky voice I'd heard at Denise's, she promised, "It will only hurt for a moment."

And then I felt the stab of sharp teeth penetrating the skin of my throat. With a panic that vibrated through my body, ringing in every cell and fiber of my being, I knew I had to fight, but I was paralyzed. I couldn't even lift a hand to wipe away the single tear that had slipped from the corner of my eye to slide down my cheek.

The one comfort I had was that Sebastian would eventually have to come back home. If I could just make it until then...

My hopes were dashed, however, when I heard another voice, a velvety tone that rose above the buzzing in my ears.

"There will be time for that later, Heather. Bring her here."

It was Sebastian.

CHAPTER TWELVE

"Sebastian?" I squeaked.

Behind me, Heather withdrew her teeth and laughed, a mirthless sound. Her warm breath tickled my ear and made me shudder.

"That's what you call him, yes."

Taking my arm in a vise grip, Heather guided me none-too-gently on into the candlelit room. Standing on the other side of the long, narrow space was Sebastian. He was leaning up against the wall beside a spiral staircase that disappeared into the darkness behind him. In one hand, he held a large book. I recognized it from the display in his office. It was the book about vampires, the one that he'd partially translated.

"Sebastian, what's going on?" I asked.

"Sweet Ridley," he said, shaking his head. "Poor sweet, clueless Ridley."

Despite the precariousness of my situation, my hackles rose at his patronizing tone. I bristled silently, waiting for him to continue, cautioning myself to keep my mouth shut.

"I could've spared you some of this if you'd only sipped from your drink, like you did that first night. Only you didn't and now, here we are."

"What is going on Sebastian?" I repeated.

Sebastian paused. "How shall I explain this?" he asked rhetorically, his question more to himself than to anyone else in the room. "Let's just say that you are a vital part of my experiment."

I gulped.

"What experiment?"

"My experiment to see if you're the one, of course."

"The one what?"

"The one for Bo."

Airflow in and out of my lungs stopped. "Bo? What's Bo got to do with this?"

"Bo has everything to do with this," Sebastian said, pushing himself away from the wall. "Haven't you figured it all out yet? Don't you know who I am?"

Sebastian strode slowly to the center of the room and stopped, facing me. A smug grin tipped one side of his mouth.

A loud sound, like a single flap, popped in the otherwise quiet room and a puff of air feathered my face. Though Sebastian's form didn't change, on the wall behind him, a shadow appeared. It was the shadow of two large wings arising from his silhouette, the span reaching from one end of the long room to the other.

"Wh-who are you?" I whispered.

"My true name is Constantine, but you may still call me Sebastian."

A thousand inconsequential things flooded my mind, as if my body's only mechanism of defense was to drown out the reality of what I was seeing, of what I knew to be true, with minutia.

"Constantine," I repeated dazedly. "But you're dead."

He laughed, a malicious snarl that made his beautiful face suddenly ugly.

"That's what they say," he muttered nonchalantly. "That's what I wanted them to say."

"But- but..." I couldn't even formulate an intelligent question. I was desperately trying to recall everything I'd heard about Constantine, to glue all the bits and pieces together into some kind of discernible picture.

Sebastian cocked his head to one side and flexed his shoulders, the shadow of wings behind him disappearing. He rolled his eyes back to me.

"Well, I was going to explain it all to you, but why not just wait for our next guest to join us?"

As if on cue, I felt the familiar tug of Bo's nearness, and while part of me was thrilled to feel his presence, the rest of me was terrified for his safety. I had to warn him.

Before I could lose my nerve or tip them off as to my intent, I lunged toward the door, surprising Heather, who lost her grip on me.

"Bo, get out of here!" I shouted at the top of my lungs.

That was all I managed to get out before a hand clamped painfully over my mouth. But it was enough. I knew Bo had heard that. His hearing was too sensitive not to have picked up on it.

"Bring her here," Sebastian commanded. "He'll come. Nothing she can say will keep him away. In fact, her shrill warning will only make him hurry, make him sloppy. I couldn't have planned it any better."

With one hand over my mouth and the other across my waist, Heather pulled me back against her, picked me up and carried me across the room to Sebastian. He tipped his head, gesturing to a place against the wall. Heather continued past him to the spot where Sebastian had been, near the stairs. She stopped, but didn't release me.

Sebastian turned back to the door, reaching behind him and pulling a long thin blade from a sheath I hadn't seen strapped to his back. He held the blade out in front of him, twisting it slightly in his grasp, the razor sharp edge catching the light and reflecting it.

I was strangely captivated by the play of the candles' flames in the gleaming silver. It was the flicker of those lights that shook me from my fascination.

A gust of wind threatened the flames and pushed the hair back from my face. I looked up and Sebastian was gone.

Next, I saw blurry streaks darting across the room, like cyclones stirring the air. I heard grunts and sounds of struggle, grappling, but still I couldn't make out any distinct shapes.

The ache in my chest and the tethers tugging at my soul assured me that Bo was in the room. It didn't matter that I couldn't see him. I felt him like I felt the hand across my face. My heart raced in fear for him, in fear for us all.

But then, with a thump that rattled the rafters and shook dust from every crack in the room, Bo appeared. He was affixed to one of the exposed wooden beams that supported the ceiling. The silver hilt of the knife was protruding from his chest—right over his heart.

Sebastian appeared next, only a fraction of a second later, standing right in front of Bo. With one quick movement, he tore Bo's shirt front open and turned to walk casually back to the center of the room, dusting his hands off as he went.

I couldn't stop the scream. It bubbled in my throat, burned in my chest, trembled on my tongue, but ultimately, it was smothered by Heather's hand.

"That ought to release some of that poison. Nasty stuff, isn't it, Bo?"

Bo was gasping and pulling at the blade, to no avail. There was no doubt that the metal had pierced his heart. As I watched, the telltale gangrenous blackness crept out from the handle and spread across Bo's chest, assuring me that there was no doubt about the poison either.

"Now," Sebastian began amicably. "Shall I make some introductions?" He looked from Bo to me and back again. No one said a word. I suspected that no one probably so much as breathed. We all waited to see what bomb Sebastian would drop.

"My name is Constantine. I am your father and you are my son. Boaz, the son of the angels."

My heart, my very soul, dropped into my shoes. Remembering the wings that had arisen from Sebastian's shadow, it made much more sense now. He was a dark angel, a fallen angel.

It's true! It's true! Dear God, help us, it's all true!

Bo and Boaz were one and the same. Bo was the son of two rebellious angels. Bo was the boy who can't be killed. He was the boy destined to kill his father.

Beneath the thin sheen of sweat that covered Bo's face and the cracks that marred its perfect texture, I saw him pale.

"My father?" It took Bo only a fraction of a minute to put it all together and, in him, I could sense a storm building. "So, you're the one…" Bo trailed off, his eyes darting toward me, only they didn't look at me. They looked behind me. "And you must be Heather."

She said nothing, though I imagined that she was smiling. She seemed devilish that way.

"Ah, is that the click-clack of puzzle pieces I hear, finally falling into place?" Sebastian mocked.

"But how? Why? Why would you hurt innocent people?" Bo managed.

"Don't be naïve. No one's innocent. The people I chose to be your 'parents' were simply the most convenient choices to fill the position, as they all have been. And the how, well, if you must know, my blood is more powerful than anything you can imagine. Feeding it to you was ridiculously easy and it made controlling your memories like child's play. And humans? Even more so. Isn't that right, Ridley?" He looked back at me and I could do nothing but stare in astonishment, mouth agape under Heather's fingers.

Sebastian turned back to Bo. "She had no idea that she was drinking my blood. You'd think that losing hours of her life might've made her suspicious, but she's just as adorably oblivious as you always have been."

I felt blood heat my cheeks as it flooded the skin of my face. I'd wondered about those couple hours I couldn't remember that night, when I'd awakened on the couch downstairs. Naively, not once had I considered Sebastian might have had something to do with it.

Idiot! I scolded myself.

"You've done this before?" Bo asked incredulously.

I could tell that Bo was having a hard time with the information, especially just having suffered such a devastating wound. It was a miracle he could think at all.

"Of course. How do you think you've spent the last few hundred years?" Sebastian chuckled, a series of sardonic barks. "Oh, that's right. Your memory is…well, it's a little faulty now. Has been for a while. I guess it's all the tampering. Not that it matters now anyway. You'll be immune to it in the future since you've had the blood of your mate, but you'll never get those memories back. Or erase the painful ones from this life."

Sebastian's eyes glowed with pleasure, his handsome face a cruel mask. He actually enjoyed torturing Bo, enjoyed telling him hurtful things and watching him squirm.

Bo closed his eyes. At first I thought he was in pain, and he was. Only this pain was of the emotional variety. He was still grieving for the only parents he'd ever known.

"And the woman who was my mother, will you kill her?"

"Not yet. But ultimately, that will be up to you."

After giving it a couple seconds to sink in, Sebastian continued. "Well," he said, clapping his hands together. "I suppose it's time to get this show on the road. That's all the time we have today for a heartfelt reunion. Now, we must get down to business. I'm sure you've heard the stories, so you know that I'm here for one thing and one thing only: to kill you."

According to Lucius's stories and the translated texts in Sebastian's office, killing Bo was an impossibility. But even so, it still terrified me to hear an angel talk about taking the life of the man that held my heart.

"Go for it," Bo ground out between labored breaths.

"Well, there is a little something that I must learn first. That's why I've asked sweet Ridley to join us," Sebastian said dramatically, sweeping his arm toward me.

"If you hurt her…" Bo spat.

"What was that?" Sebastian cupped his ear theatrically. "I couldn't quite make that out. I guess it's the silver dagger sticking out of your heart. Makes it hard to understand you."

"I'll rip you apart," Bo huffed weakly.

"Mmm, let's save that for another time, shall we?"

Sebastian walked back toward me, stopping at my side.

"She's quite stunning, you know," he said, reaching out to take a lock of my hair that had fallen down across my breast and twirl it around his finger. "It must be a father-son thing, the love we have for beautiful women." Sebastian faced me full on and said quietly, "And their love for us."

Reaching around me to a small table that sat to my right, Sebastian took hold of an oddly familiar wooden stake. I don't know why it seemed like I'd seen it before, but I was certain I recognized it. He hefted it in his hand, as if testing the weight, and then he turned and hurled it across the room at Bo.

With a loud thump, the stake buried its tip in Bo's side, to the right of his navel, evidently penetrating his body to embed in the wide beam behind him. When he cried out in agony, it felt as if I had been impaled as well. His pain lanced through me in a physical way, piercing my guts like a scalpel.

"No!" I screamed, but once more it was smothered by Heather's hand.

Sebastian faced me again. "Not enough? Would you like to see more?"

With that, he reached for another stake and, in one fluid motion, pivoted and threw it unerringly at Bo. This one landed deep in his left thigh.

Bo must've gasped in anguish and gotten choked. He coughed and sputtered, blood spewing from his mouth.

The room swayed before my eyes so I squeezed them shut, unable to watch, unable to bear his torture.

Viciously strong fingers grabbed my face and my eyes flew open. Sebastian was glaring down at me, his lips thin and set in a straight, angry line.

"More?"

In horror, I watched as he took yet another stake from the table and flung it at Bo. It penetrated his knee with a splintering sound. I knew it wasn't the stake giving way; it was Bo's bone.

"Oh, God, please," I mumbled behind Heather's hand.

Sebastian turned back to me, rage etched on every sharp angle of his face.

"God? You dare to call on Him in my presence?"

Furiously, Sebastian grabbed another thick chunk of the familiar whittled wood from the table. I shook my head desperately, but still he turned and launched it at Bo. I watched his arm extend and his hand release the stake, each motion slow and exaggerated, as if he was moving in molasses. I saw every rotation the projectile made on its way to Bo. I heard the hiss of Bo's breath as it neared him. I felt the way he braced himself against the pain, felt it as surely as if it were happening to me.

As the wood buried itself in Bo's right shoulder, blood spurted out, droplets flying through the air and peppering his gorgeous face. I surveyed his broken and bloodied body, my heart wrenching inside my tight chest. The anguish I felt for Bo began to meld with another sensation, one that I'd felt before. It was more than fear, more than love, more than helplessness or anger. It was a sweet hurt that I immediately recognized and embraced.

Yes, the terror was there and the rage, but also the feeling that an old friend — a trusted friend, a powerful friend — had arrived to lend a hand. And with one shaky breath, I let her have her way.

Inside me, she built more quickly this time—the familiar pressure in my chest that oozed into my stomach, where it churned angrily. Within seconds, she had flooded my veins, mingling with my blood and carrying my tie with Bo to the surface, where it throbbed and pulsed just beneath the covering of my flesh.

I knew what was coming next, and when it did, I welcomed the razors that sliced at me, welcomed the exquisite agony of my skin pulling away to let free the power that prowled inside me. I shook with it, trembled with it. It vibrated through me, forcing Heather's hand away from my mouth.

I closed my eyes as a glorious laugh spilled from between my lips. It was followed by the scream that had been brewing in my chest. I felt my love for Bo pouring through me—the desperation of it, the overwhelming force of it. It promised to save us both and I let it flow.

When I opened my eyes, they found Bo's like a magnet. My body, my life, my soul was attached and attracted to him, finding him with an undeniable certainty.

Through the heavy slits of his weary lids, Bo's ebony orbs watched me. From across the room, I saw in them understanding.

I turned my gaze on Sebastian, ready to unleash the wrath that swelled within me. He stood near the stairs, with Heather by his side, but when I saw him, my anger died instantaneously. I couldn't bring myself to hurt him as he was.

He held Lilly in his arms.

I looked at her peaceful, still-sleeping face and then back up to Sebastian's. He was wearing a smile that reeked of satisfaction, one that silently proclaimed his victory.

"Bravo," he said facetiously. "You've just proved that you are the one."

As the anger and the power burned off, my mind reeled with confusion.

"What? I don't understand."

"You've given me the one true weakness of the boy who can't be killed: his soul mate."

Far beneath all the tragedy of what was going on, a bright light of pure pleasure beamed within me, hoping upon hope that he was right, but only about the soul mate part. Then, quickly, I forced my focus back to the present.

"But I'm not his weakness."

"Oh, but you are. Heather here has made sure that you have enough venom in your blood to turn ten beautiful young girls into monsters, which leaves Bo here with a decision to make."

My blood ran ice cold and drained away from my face. What had she done? What had he done?

I felt panic clawing its way up inside me, threatening to have its way, but I tamped it down, knowing it was something I couldn't afford to worry about right now.

I looked back at Bo. He was glaring murderously at Sebastian from his place against the wooden support beam. Judging by the look in his eye, I was the only one who failed to understand what Sebastian was talking about.

"What decision?"

"You're soon to be a vampire, sweet Ridley. Bo here is smart enough to know that if he kills me, he will become mortal, and that means that he'd leave the love of his life to walk the earth for eternity...alone. Once he attains mortality, there is no going back. Your misery, your heartache, your loneliness—it would all be his fault."

My head swam as if it were filled with hazy liquid and nausea sloshed in my stomach at the mere prospect of the future that he described. I shook my head, literally putting my fingertips to my temples in an effort to control what was happening inside it. And then, with a determination I didn't believe myself capable of, I violently shoved those selfish thoughts aside.

"And what makes you so sure that I won't kill you? Maybe I'm the weapon that will take your traitorous life."

"Well, if that's a theory you wish to test, then I suppose there's not much I can do about it. But let me warn you of this, Ridley. If you were to try such a thing, I would be forced to take innocent Lilly's life."

I gasped.

"You would do that to your own child?"

"You ask that when I just put a dagger through the heart of my beloved son? But the answer is yes, I would it again, only I wouldn't have to."

"What? Why not?"

"Because Lilly isn't my daughter."

"Then who's—"

"Lilly is more closely related to you than she is to me," Sebastian interrupted gleefully. He was obviously alluding to a secret juicy enough to find great pleasure in revealing.

"What's that supposed to mean?"

"I don't suppose it will hurt to tell you that my Iofiel has found out some very interesting, very valuable information in the past few hundred years. For instance, did you know that the blood of a child born a vampire holds unique power?"

I shook my head. "No, but what does this have to do with—"

"With you? Well, I would've thought that your niece's life might mean something to you—the last little piece of your sister—but I guess I could've misjudged you."

"My niece? But I don't have a- a..."

I trailed off as silver blue eyes floated through my head. A bell-like laugh and gleaming auburn locks, only these didn't belong to Lilly. They belonged to Izzy.

"But Izzy died. And so did the baby," I muttered quietly, still befuddled.

"Did Bo happen to mention that his 'mother' worked at the hospital?"

My mouth dropped open, working fruitlessly to wrap my lips around words that I couldn't find.

"You're lying," I whispered.

"Heather, let's give Ridley here a little memento of what she stands to lose...again."

From her pocket, Heather pulled out a silver rectangle and tossed it to me. It landed on the floor with a clatter and skidded to a halt in front of me. I looked down and recognized Izzy's cell phone where it lay at my feet. This was why it had never been recovered. Sebastian had stolen the phone when he'd turned the baby inside her womb.

"Amazing what the blood of an angel, a vampire angel, can do for a fetus, isn't it?"

I had nothing to say to that. I let the tense silence stretch on as I stared numbly at the phone, searching for some other kind of explanation, but finding none.

Sebastian voice penetrated the quiet like a sharp arrow, finding its target in the center of my chest.

"Know this," Sebastian said, his tone turning deadly serious. "I am more powerful than you can imagine. I have beings at my disposal that can bring you and Lilly pain that there is no description for, creatures much worse than Lars.

This is the only warning you'll get: don't try to find me or you'll spend the rest of eternity regretting it."

He paused to drive his point home, his eyes boring holes first into Bo and then into me. Then, in a swirl of dust, he disappeared, taking Heather and Lilly with him.

CHAPTER THIRTEEN

A silence fell over the room, a silence filled with fears so loud I could barely hear myself think. The loud patter of Bo's blood dripping into the puddles on the floor finally roused me from my dumbfounded state.

I hurried to his side, my hands flitting from knife handle to stake and back again. I had no idea how to help him, what to do first.

"The knife. Get the knife out," he groaned weakly.

Wrapping my trembling fingers around the cool hilt, I pulled as hard as I could, but it didn't budge. Inhaling, I held my breath and tried again. Nothing.

"Bo, I can't get it out. What are we going to do?"

His chest heaved with his efforts just to breathe and remain conscious.

"We'll try together," he said, his cooling fingers brushing mine as they curled around the hilt, too. "On the count of three. One. Two. Three."

I pulled as hard as I could, as Bo did and, thankfully, the dagger's tip sprang free of the wood behind Bo's back and slipped out. I pitched it onto the floor and turned my attention to the stakes that protruded from Bo like pins from a pin cushion.

I began with the one in his knee. I could see that it was not embedded in the support beam, so I grabbed it and yanked, pulling it easily from Bo's body. Blood began to flow from the open wound.

Of the three remaining stakes, I was dismayed to learn that only one was not stuck in the wood behind Bo. The one at his shoulder had caught the edge of the beam, but I could see the tip sticking out of Bo's body. It was clearly not embedded. Bo's wide shoulders had saved him from being further pinned to the thick column.

After I'd pulled that one out, I looked once more at the other two stakes. I was afraid that the one in his thigh had gone through Bo's bone to stick into the wood. The one in his side was stuck as well.

I noticed that the skin of Bo's side was becoming less apparent as his injuries, coupled with the stress of the whole ordeal, burned through the blood he'd fed upon. The poisonous coloring had not receded either, and I knew that wasn't helping his condition. I knew I had to hurry.

"Bo, you're going to have to help me with these last two, ok?"

Bo nodded his head feebly. His fingers dropped to the stake at his side. "On three."

On the count of three, we tried to remove the dense piece of wood, but it didn't budge.

"Let's try again," I suggested.

Bo shook his head this time. "I can't. I'm losing blood too fast."

"Then drink from me."

Again, he shook his head. "No. The more blood you lose, the faster you'll turn."

I couldn't help the pause. I couldn't help the fact that Drew's tortured face flitted through my head as he begged for us to kill him. He would rather have died than live as a vampire.

I shook my head against the thoughts. They had no place here now. My fate was sealed. Fear and regret couldn't matter. They no longer held any sway.

"I don't care. We have to get you out of here."

"No, Ridley. It's too fast."

To my way of thinking at that moment, ever was too fast.

"What difference does it make?" Even as I asked the question, I felt a pang of sickening dread.

"Loving me has cost you so much. The least I can do is give you a few more days," Bo said miserably.

Having a few more days of humanity felt like a stay of execution to me, but I couldn't tell Bo that. He needed me and that was all that mattered.

"A few more days doesn't matter. Here," I said, picking the long thin knife up off the floor.

I stared at the blade, slick with Bo's blood.

Giving my flesh to Bo, my blood to Bo, was quite different than purposely slicing my arm open with a sharp knife. Reluctantly, I looked back up at him. He was watching me, his eyes already turning that milky green in his disappearing face.

"Ridley, you don't have to do this."

"I know."

Closing my eyes, I drew the razor-sharp edge across the tender skin of my wrist. I bit my lip against the sting of pain.

I opened my eyes to Bo's pale ones watching me closely, hungrily. But behind the hunger was pain—the pain of what was to become of me, the pain of what he felt like his love had cost me, the pain of having little choice other than to drink from me, to take from me.

I straightened my spine and smiled. "Besides, this is the last time you'll get to taste this human blood," I said pluckily, determined to hide my distress from him. I held my wrist to his lips. "Here, for old times' sake."

The battle waging inside Bo was plain to see. It was there in his tormented eyes, in his forlorn expression. But in the end, his thirst won out. His need. As his teeth pierced my skin, holding me tightly to him, I realized that I would soon know what that overwhelming hunger felt like. Soon, I'd require blood to live, too.

For the first time since she'd bitten me, I felt the fiery burn of Heather's venom radiating from my neck down into my chest. It was killing off all that made me human, changing me forever, and now, forever had a much different meaning.

Pushing those thoughts aside, I closed my eyes on the world around me and concentrated on the feel of Bo's soft lips and cool tongue as they moved against my skin.

Time does this funny thing where it sort of disappears when Bo's feeding from me, so I don't know how much had elapsed when he released my wrist. I felt myself sway and his hand slide around my waist to steady me. I felt my lips curve with the pleasure of being wrapped in his strong arms. For all of eternity, there was no place I'd rather be. But if Bo fulfilled his destiny, it was the one place eternity couldn't offer.

****

That was the last memory I had before I ended up in the woods, running for my life, fleeing from the vampires. Now I was stuck in a hole in the forest with no one around to help me out.

All my senses reached out and took in my surroundings. I could still smell the dankness of the earth that enveloped me. I opened eyes I didn't even remember closing and looked around. The darkness was almost complete. I could barely make out the mouth of the shaft into which I'd fallen.

I was cold and achy and I knew I was hurt. Probably very badly. Everything was throbbing dully, as if to the beat of my heart. But strangely, considering that it was my legs that had taken the brunt of my fall, it was my chest that hurt the worst. It felt like everything behind my sternum was shriveling up and dying. It was excruciating, so painful in fact that I was amazed I was still conscious.

And my throat hurt, too. It burned like I'd sipped acid. My mouth was dry as cotton, but I swallowed what little saliva I had. It did nothing to relieve the discomfort. The fire persisted.

A familiar sound teased my ears. I stilled, listening as closely as I could. It was Bo's voice, pouring over my raw senses like warm honey. He was calling my name, over and over. But he sounded far away, too far to be coming for me.

I tried to open my mouth to call out to him, but no words left my tongue. I felt something warm on my cheek and the walls of the shaft began to shake, dirt crumbling from the sides and sprinkling my face and hair. I felt the panic of the world falling in all around me as bigger chunks of earth started to come away from the sides of the tube.

Again, I heard Bo's voice and the warmth at my cheek became an annoying tap. I reached up to brush at my face and I felt something there. It was a hand.

A terrified scream gurgled in my burning throat as I flailed my arms, slapping at the air around me, at whatever was touching me.

"Ridley," I heard Bo say. I stopped moving, reaching out for his voice and holding on tight.

"Bo?" I managed, my tongue sticking to the roof of my mouth.

"I'm here," he whispered.

"Where? Where are you?" I squinted into the darkness, searching desperately for his face in the tiny circle that was the mouth of the hole, far above me.

"Right here, Ridley."

I felt the hand at my cheek again. When I reached out, I could feel Bo's fingers, his wrist, his arm. But still, I saw nothing.

"It's ok. You're ok," he said softly, his voice right at my ear.

I reached out with my other hand and I could feel Bo's chest in front of me, where he leaned in to speak to me.

"Bo, I can't see you." I felt an irrational fear tremble in my gut.

"Open your eyes, baby."

"They're open."

"No, they're not, Ridley. Just open your eyes."

"I'm trying. I can't see you."

My voice quivered with emotion, my chin drawing up, tears wetting my lashes.

"Come to me, Ridley. Wherever you're at, come back here to me."

Bo's lips brushed mine and a calm stole over me.

"Bo, what's happening?"

"You're turning too fast, baby. You're hallucinating. You need to wake up."

"Turning? What?"

The dirt walls finally fell, giving way to reality as it rushed in. My lids fluttered against the bright, white light that blinded me. Holding my hand up to shield my face, I squinted. A sob clogged my throat when I was able to make out the glorious sight of Bo hovering over me.

He pulled me up into his arms and buried his face in my neck. I inhaled, the odor of damp earth replaced by Bo's fresh, tangy scent.

Gingerly, I opened my eyes wider. The ceiling of Sebastian's den hung above me, the same one I'd awakened to the night I'd lost time. Bo's hair tickled my cheek and I could hear the steady thump of his heart.

A gushing, flowing sound interrupted my cataloging of my surroundings. It seemed to be punctuated by Bo's heartbeat. I listened more closely, but couldn't identify it as something familiar, as something I'd heard before. And then Bo's words came back to me, words he'd just spoken.

You're turning too fast, baby.

The pain in my chest worsened, nearly stealing my breath, and the swishing noise grew louder and louder. My throat seemed to seize around a knot of dry dust lodged there and I leaned back to look at Bo. Something was wrong.

I pushed at Bo's shoulders and he obliged by pulling away from me. My fingers were still twisted in his hair, which meant that my arms were stretched out in front of me. Only they weren't. I fisted my hands, feeling the undeniable tickle of Bo's hair against my palms. That's when it all hit home.

My arms were invisible. I was invisible. Because I was turning into a vampire.

TO BE CONTINUED IN BOOK 3
BLOOD LIKE POISON: TO KILL AN ANGEL

A WORD

A few times in life, I've found myself in a position of such love and gratitude that saying THANK YOU seems trite, like it's just not enough. That is the position that I find myself in now when it comes to you, my readers. You are the sole reason that my dream of being a writer has come true. I knew that it would be gratifying and wonderful to finally have a job that I loved so much, but I had no idea that it would be outweighed and outshined by the unimaginable pleasure that I get from hearing that you love my work, that it's touched you in some way or that your life seems a little bit better for having read it. So it is from the depths of my soul, from the very bottom of my heart that I say I simply cannot THANK YOU enough. I've added this note to all my stories with the link to a blog post that I really hope you'll take a minute to read. It is a true and sincere expression of my humble appreciation. I love each and every one of you and you'll never know what your many encouraging posts, comments and e-mails have meant to me.

http://mleightonbooks.blogspot.com/2011/06/when-thanks-is-not-enough.html

ABOUT THE AUTHOR

M. Leighton is a native of Ohio, but she relocated to the warmer climates of the South, where she can be near the water all summer and miss the snow all winter. Possessed of an overactive imagination from early in her childhood, Michelle finally found an acceptable outlet for her fantastical visions: writing fiction. Five of Michelle's novels can now be found on Amazon, as well as several other sites. She's currently working on sequels, though her mind continues to churn out new ideas, exciting plots and quirky characters. Pick one up and enjoy a wild ride through the twists and turns of her vivid imagination.

OTHER BOOKS BY M. LEIGHTON
Caterpillar
Madly & Wolfhardt
The Reaping
Wiccan

WHERE TO FIND MICHELLE
Blog: http://mleightonbooks.blogspot.com
Facebook: M. Leighton Author Page
Twitter: mleightonbooks
Goodreads: M. Leighton, Author

CONTACT ME
m.leighton.books@gmail.com

Made in the USA
Lexington, KY
31 October 2011